To SpongeBob's #1 Fan:

You are holding in your hands the first-EVER collection of SpongeBob comics. Pretty cool, huh? Some of these comics are more than ten years old, while some are brand-spanking-new. But all of these comics were created for *Nick Magazine*, mostly by the same artists who write and draw so many of the *SpongeBob* episodes you know and love.

That's where I come in. My name is Sherm Cohen, and I'm one of the *SpongeBob SquarePants* storyboard artists who worked on these comic stories. Now, some of you might be wondering, "What's a storyboard artist?" Well, a storyboard artist sketches the pictures for a *SpongeBob* cartoon, the first step in bringing a cartoon to life.

A comic is sort of like a storyboard before it gets animated for TV, except that a comic has word balloons, captions, sound effects, and tons of color! Storyboard artists can have loads of fun with comics because comics don't follow the same strict guidelines as TV. We can shake things up by using big panels and little panels. We can make a comic into a four-panel-long joke, or a ten-page adventure epic. And we can use all kinds of drawing styles— everything from the classic version of our favorite talking sponge to superfunky styles that make Bikini Bottom look crazy!

This collection combines comics of all shapes, sizes, lengths, and art styles . . . all brought to you by a bunch of cartoonists who love to tell funny stories.

These comics began life the same way a TV cartoon does: A handful of cartoonists sit around a table and toss ideas around until we find one that's full of funny possibilities and cool things to draw. For example, what would happen if SpongeBob got the hiccups and just couldn't stop? That little idea began to turn into an epic adventure when SpongeBob's creator, Stephen Hillenburg, suggested that Mr. Krabs might banish SpongeBob to a mythical place called Hiccup Island! My pal Derek Drymon suggested a journey to a spooky island haunted by the Flying Dutchman! I couldn't wait to get home and start sketching out the story while those images were flying around inside my head.

I had a great time drawing that story, and I'm really glad you'll have a chance to read that tale here, along with the rest of the best of the SpongeBob comic stories.

Enjoy!

Sherm Cohen
Storyboard Artist (one of many!)
and Storyboard Supervisor
for *SpongeBob SquarePants* (Seasons 1–4)

NICKELODEON
SpongeBob SquarePants

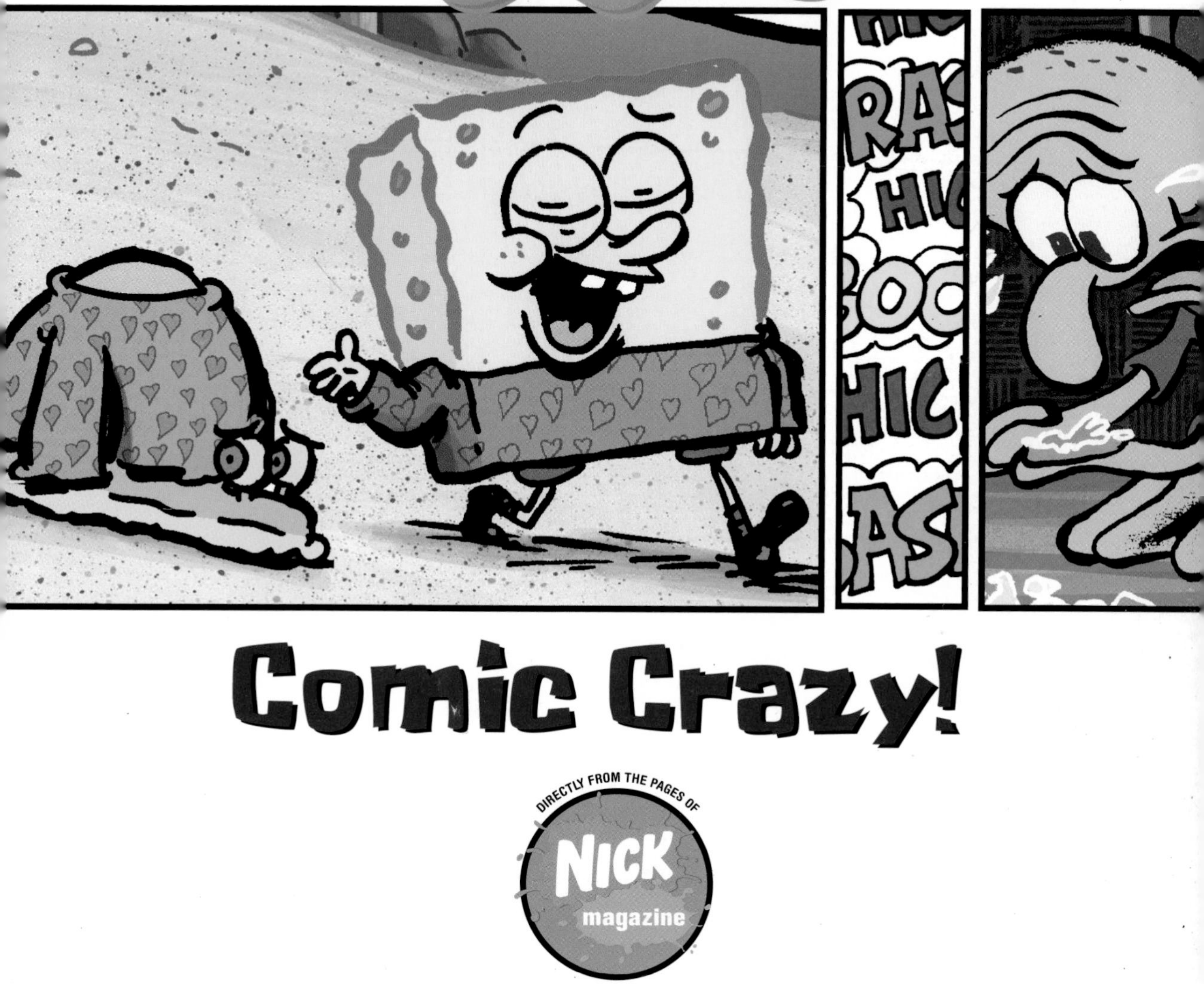

Comic Crazy!

DIRECTLY FROM THE PAGES OF NICK magazine

SIMON SPOTLIGHT/NICKELODEON
New York London Toronto Sydney

Stephen Hillenburg

Based on the TV series *SpongeBob SquarePants*® created by Stephen Hillenburg as seen on Nickelodeon®

SIMON SPOTLIGHT

An imprint of Simon & Schuster Children's Publishing Division

1230 Avenue of the Americas, New York, New York 10020

© 2009 Viacom International Inc. All rights reserved. NICKELODEON, *SpongeBob SquarePants*, and all related titles, logos, and characters are registered trademarks of Viacom International Inc. Created by Stephen Hillenburg.

All rights reserved, including the right of reproduction in whole or in part in any form.

SIMON SPOTLIGHT and colophon are registered trademarks of Simon & Schuster, Inc.

Manufactured in the United States of America

4 6 8 10 9 7 5

ISBN: 978-1-4169-8343-9

1209 WOR

"Prize Inside": Story, art, and lettering by Graham Annable. Coloring by Sno Cone Studios. "Hiccup! And Away!": Plot: Paul Tibbet. Script, art, and lettering: Sherm Cohen. Coloring: Digital Chameleon. Special thanks to: Stephen Hillenburg and Derek Drymon. "Just Desserts": Story, art, and lettering: C.H. Greenblatt. Coloring: Sno Cone Studios. "Krusty Krab Cleanup": Story: Paul Tibbit. Pencils: Mark O'Hare. Inks: Sherm Cohen. Coloring: Nick Jennings. "Dollars and Scents": Story, art, and lettering: C.H. Greenblatt. Coloring: Sno Cone Studios. "Left Out": Plot: Sam Henderson. Script, pencils, and inks: Jay Lender. Coloring: Digital Chameleon. Lettering: Sherm Cohen. "Best Fiend": Story, art, and lettering: C.H. Greenblatt. Coloring: Digital Chameleon. "Make that BigPants": Story: Walt Dohm, Art: Jay Lender, Lettering: Sherm Cohen, Coloring: Digital Chameleon. "Gone Jellyfishing": Story: Derek Drymon and Sherm Cohen. Pencils: Scott Roberts. Inks and lettering: Vince Deporter. Coloring: Digital Chameleon. "The Hole at the Bottom of the Sea": Story, art, and lettering: Sherm Cohen. Coloring: Digital Chameleon. "Dressed for Distress": Story, art, and lettering: C.H. Greenblatt. Coloring: Sno Cone Studios.

Special thanks to Stu Chaifetz. *Nick Magazine* SpongeBob comic staff: Andrew Brisman, Chris Duffy, Laura Galen, Tim Jones, Frank Pittarese, David Roman, Tina Strasberg, Catherine Tutrone, and Paul Tutrone. *Nick Magazine* would like to thank Stephen Hillenburg, Derek Drymon, and Sherm Cohen.

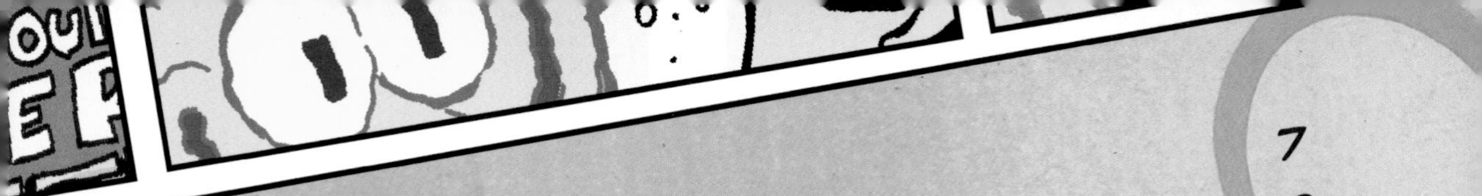

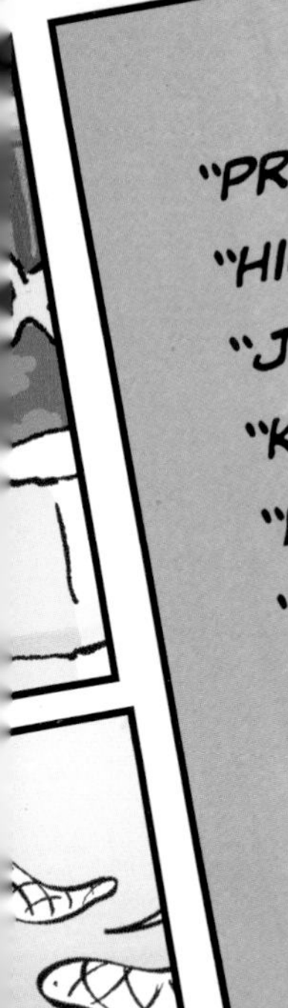

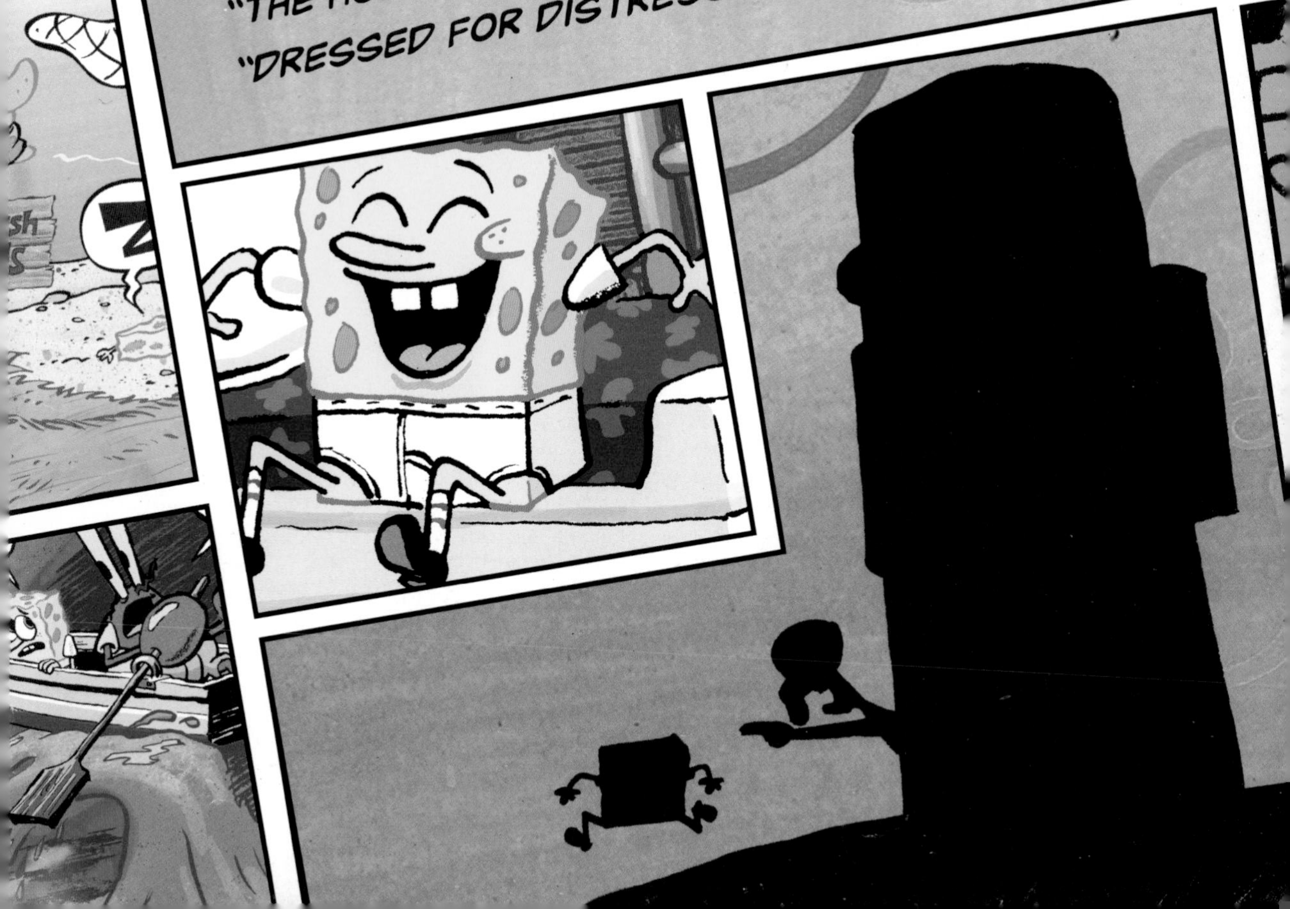

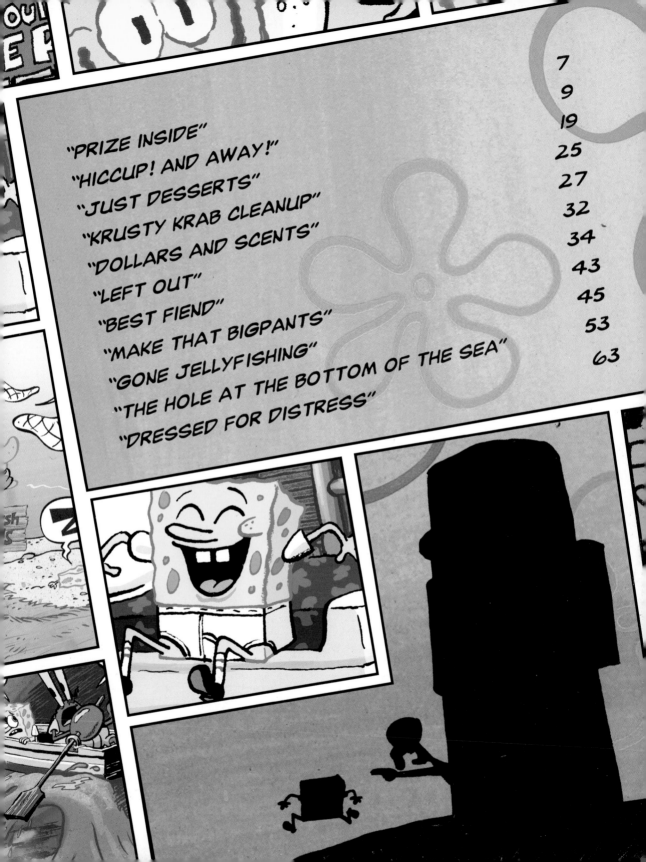

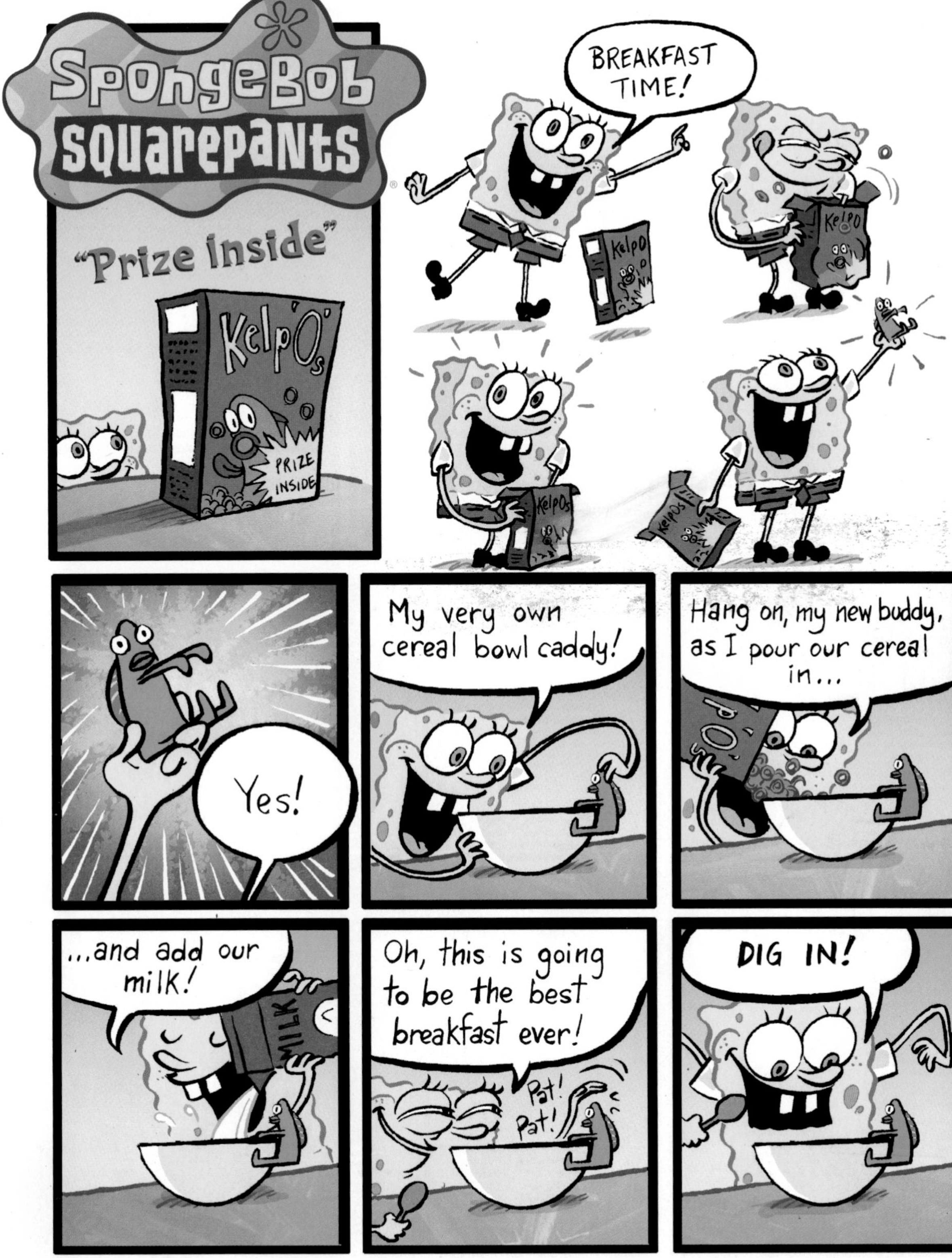

SpongeBob SquarePants
"Prize Inside"
Kelp O's
PRIZE INSIDE
BREAKFAST TIME!
Yes!
My very own cereal bowl caddy!
Hang on, my new buddy, as I pour our cereal in...
...and add our milk!
MILK
Oh, this is going to be the best breakfast ever!
Pat! Pat!
DIG IN!

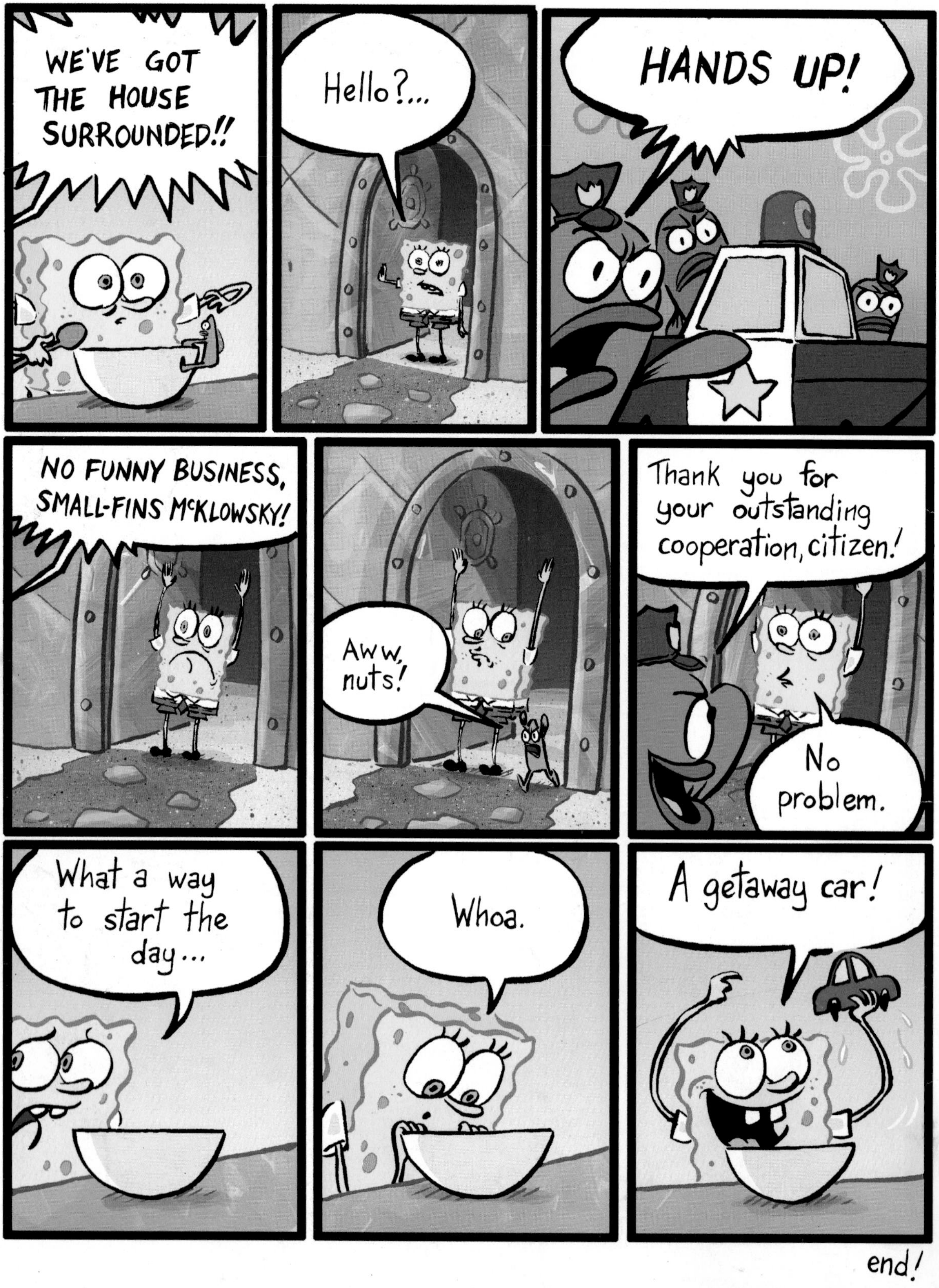

WE'VE GOT THE HOUSE SURROUNDED!!
Hello?...
HANDS UP!
NO FUNNY BUSINESS, SMALL-FINS McKLOWSKY!
Aww, nuts!
Thank you for your outstanding cooperation, citizen!
No problem.
What a way to start the day...
Whoa.
A getaway car!
end!

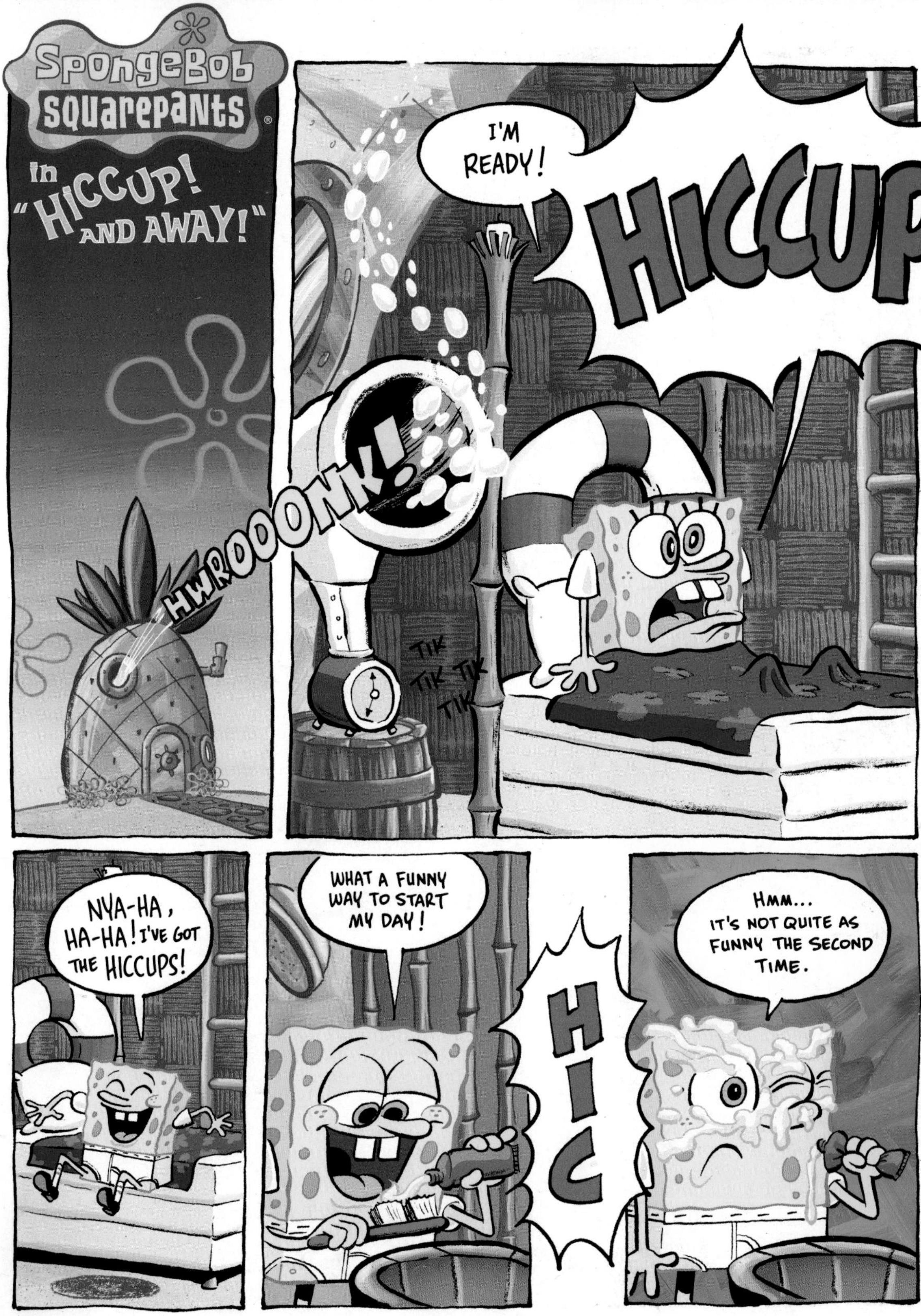
SpongeBob SquarePants®
in "HICCUP! AND AWAY!"
HWROOOONK!!
TIK TIK TIK TIK
I'M READY!
HICCUP
NYA-HA, HA-HA! I'VE GOT THE HICCUPS!
WHAT A FUNNY WAY TO START MY DAY!
HIC
HMM... IT'S NOT QUITE AS FUNNY THE SECOND TIME.

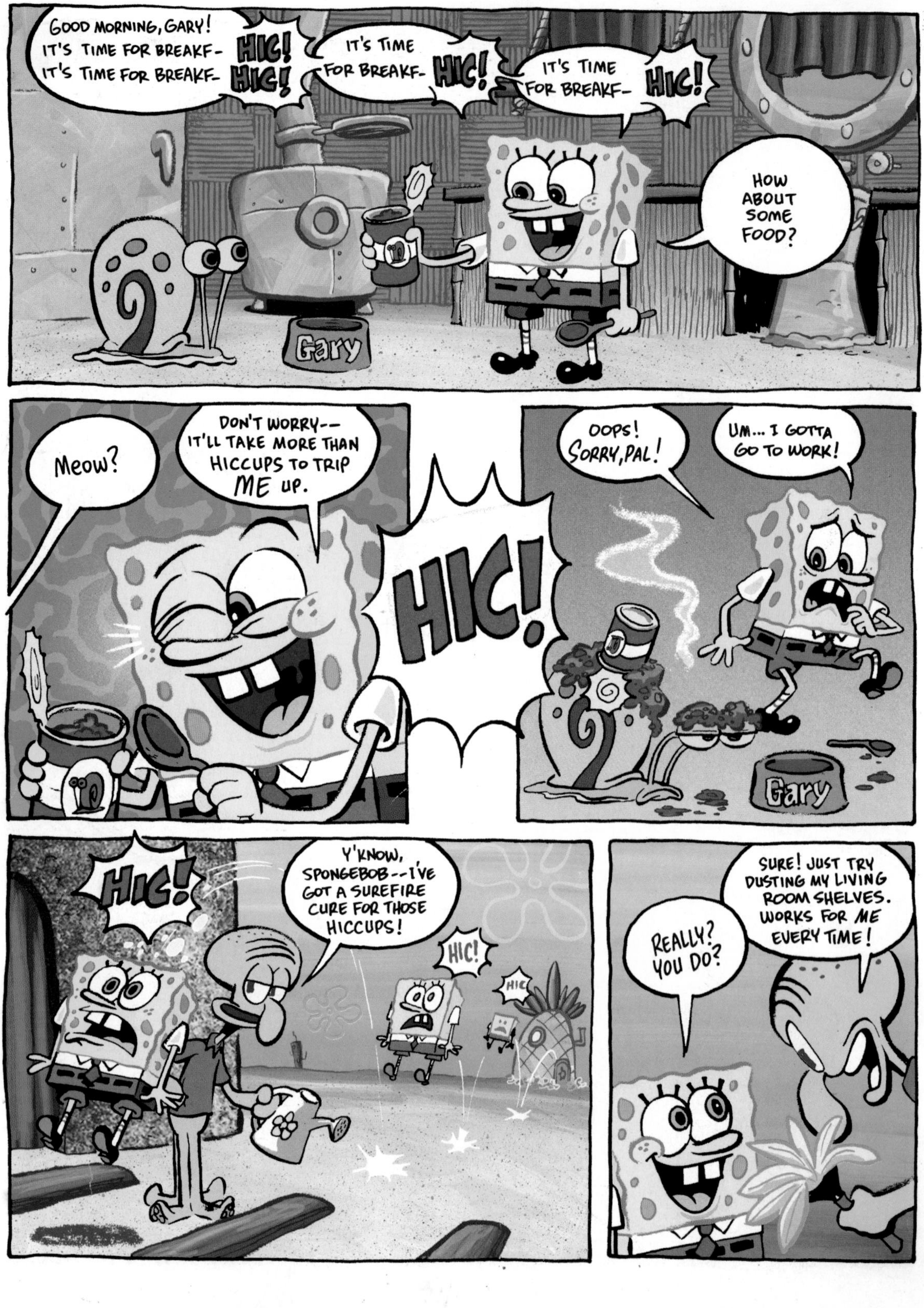
GOOD MORNING, GARY! IT'S TIME FOR BREAKF- HIC! IT'S TIME FOR BREAKF- HIC!
IT'S TIME FOR BREAKF- HIC!
IT'S TIME FOR BREAKF- HIC!
HOW ABOUT SOME FOOD?
Gary
Meow?
DON'T WORRY-- IT'LL TAKE MORE THAN HICCUPS TO TRIP ME UP.
HIC!
OOPS! SORRY, PAL!
UM... I GOTTA GO TO WORK!
Gary
HIC!
Y'KNOW, SPONGEBOB--I'VE GOT A SUREFIRE CURE FOR THOSE HICCUPS!
HIC!
HIC
REALLY? YOU DO?
SURE! JUST TRY DUSTING MY LIVING ROOM SHELVES. WORKS FOR ME EVERY TIME!

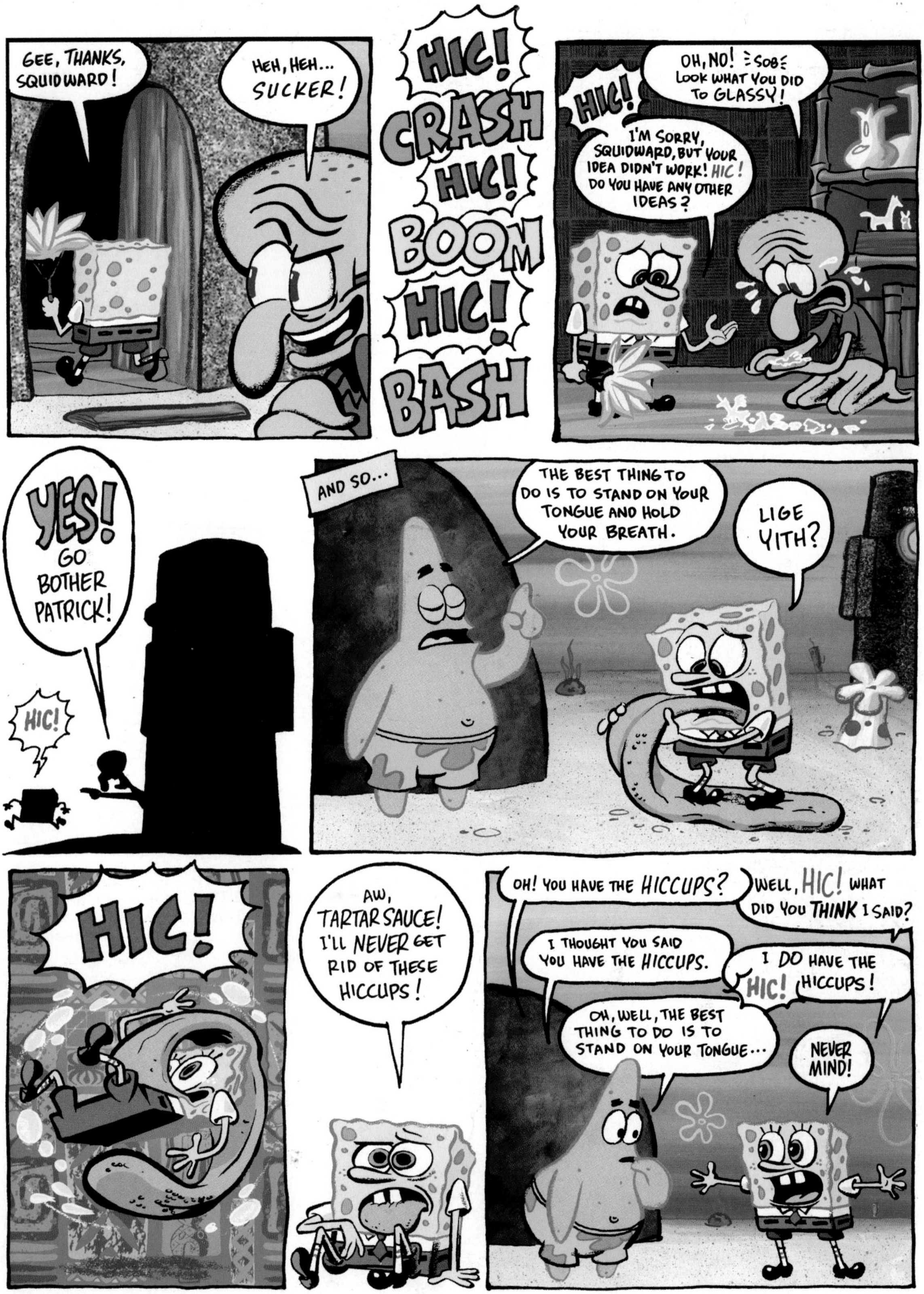

GEE, THANKS, SQUIDWARD!
HEH, HEH... SUCKER!
HIC!
CRASH
HIC!
BOOM
HIC!
BASH
HIC!
OH, NO! SOB LOOK WHAT YOU DID TO GLASSY!
I'M SORRY, SQUIDWARD, BUT YOUR IDEA DIDN'T WORK! HIC! DO YOU HAVE ANY OTHER IDEAS?
YES! GO BOTHER PATRICK!
HIC!
AND SO...
THE BEST THING TO DO IS TO STAND ON YOUR TONGUE AND HOLD YOUR BREATH.
LIGE YITH?
HIC!
AW, TARTAR SAUCE! I'LL NEVER GET RID OF THESE HICCUPS!
OH! YOU HAVE THE HICCUPS?
WELL, HIC! WHAT DID YOU THINK I SAID?
I THOUGHT YOU SAID YOU HAVE THE HICCUPS.
I DO HAVE THE HIC! HICCUPS!
OH, WELL, THE BEST THING TO DO IS TO STAND ON YOUR TONGUE...
NEVER MIND!

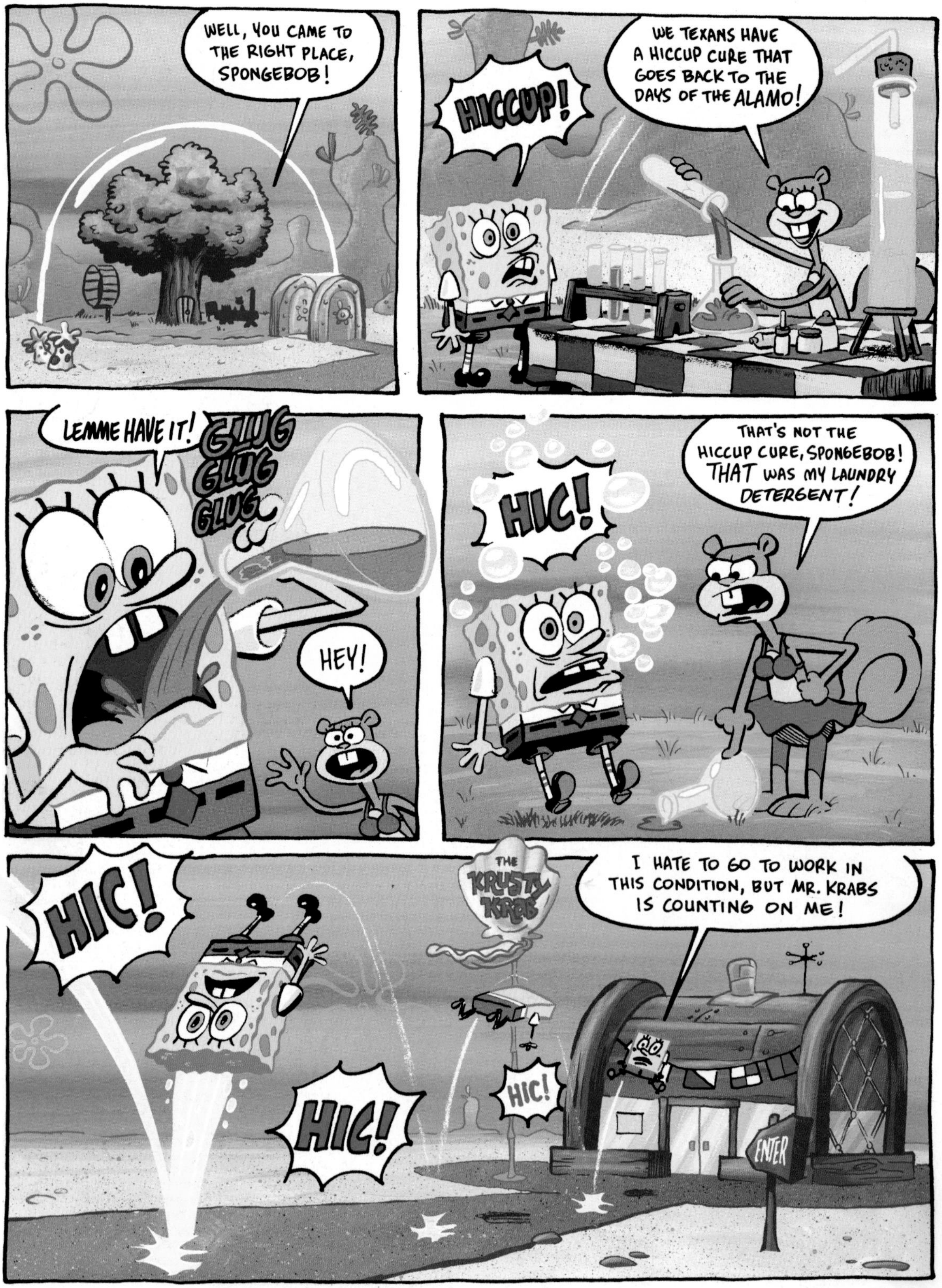

WELL, YOU CAME TO THE RIGHT PLACE, SPONGEBOB!
HICCUP!
WE TEXANS HAVE A HICCUP CURE THAT GOES BACK TO THE DAYS OF THE ALAMO!
LEMME HAVE IT!
GLUG GLUG GLUG
HEY!
HIC!
THAT'S NOT THE HICCUP CURE, SPONGEBOB! THAT WAS MY LAUNDRY DETERGENT!
HIC!
THE KRUSTY KRAB
I HATE TO GO TO WORK IN THIS CONDITION, BUT MR. KRABS IS COUNTING ON ME!
HIC!
HIC!
ENTER

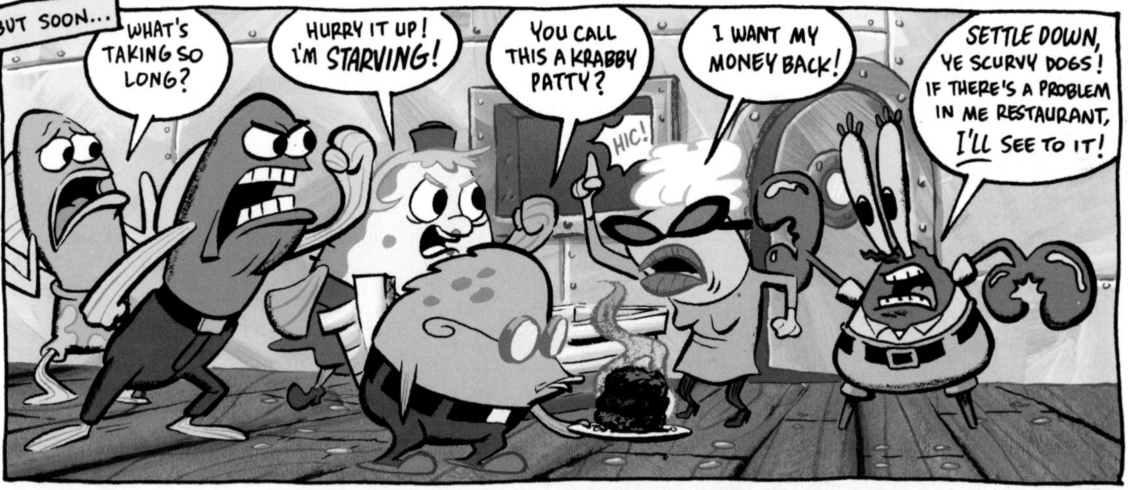
BUT SOON...
WHAT'S TAKING SO LONG?
HURRY IT UP! I'M STARVING!
YOU CALL THIS A KRABBY PATTY?
HIC!
I WANT MY MONEY BACK!
SETTLE DOWN, YE SCURVY DOGS! IF THERE'S A PROBLEM IN ME RESTAURANT, I'LL SEE TO IT!

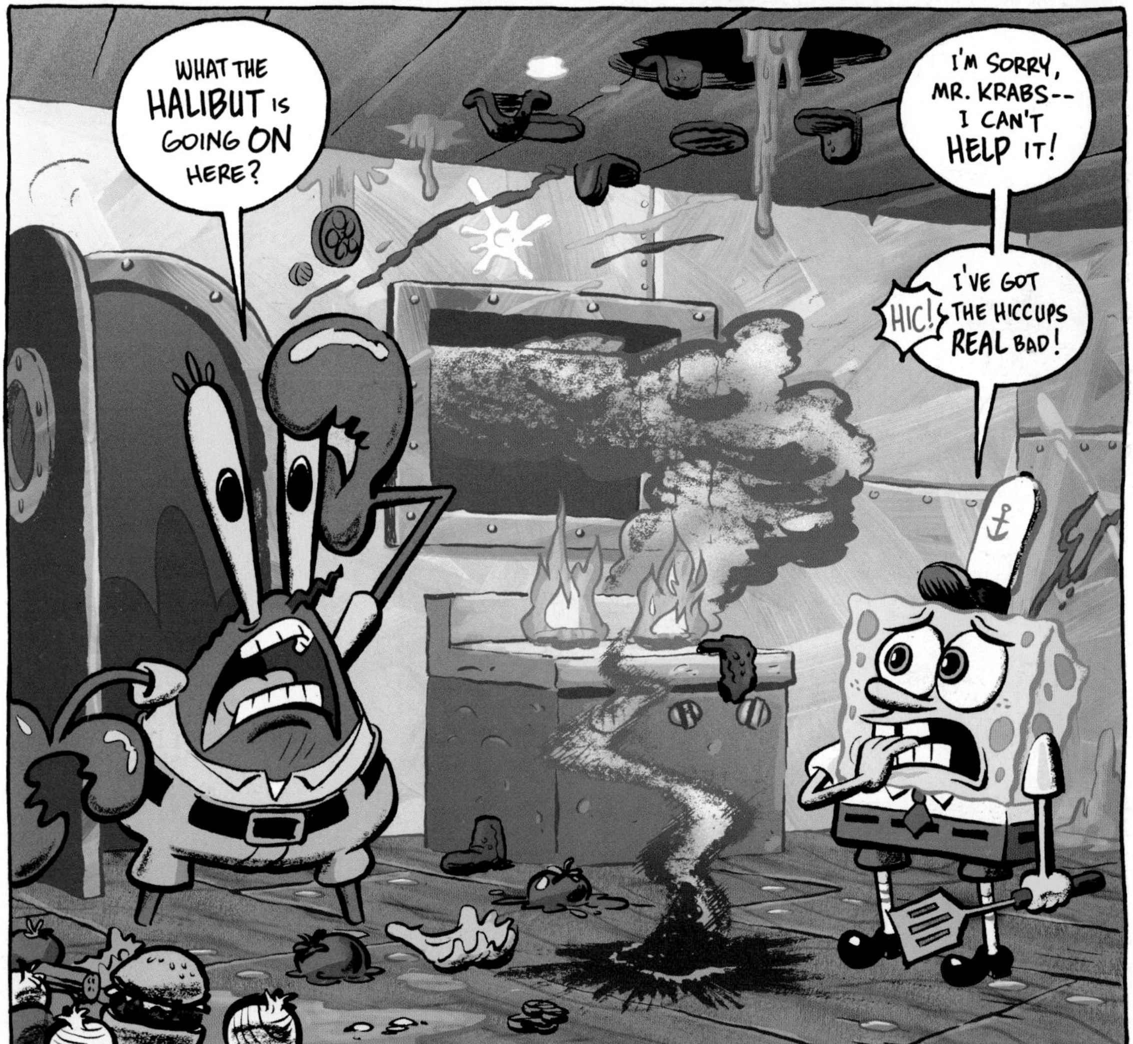
WHAT THE HALIBUT IS GOING ON HERE?
I'M SORRY, MR. KRABS-- I CAN'T HELP IT!
HIC!
I'VE GOT THE HICCUPS REAL BAD!

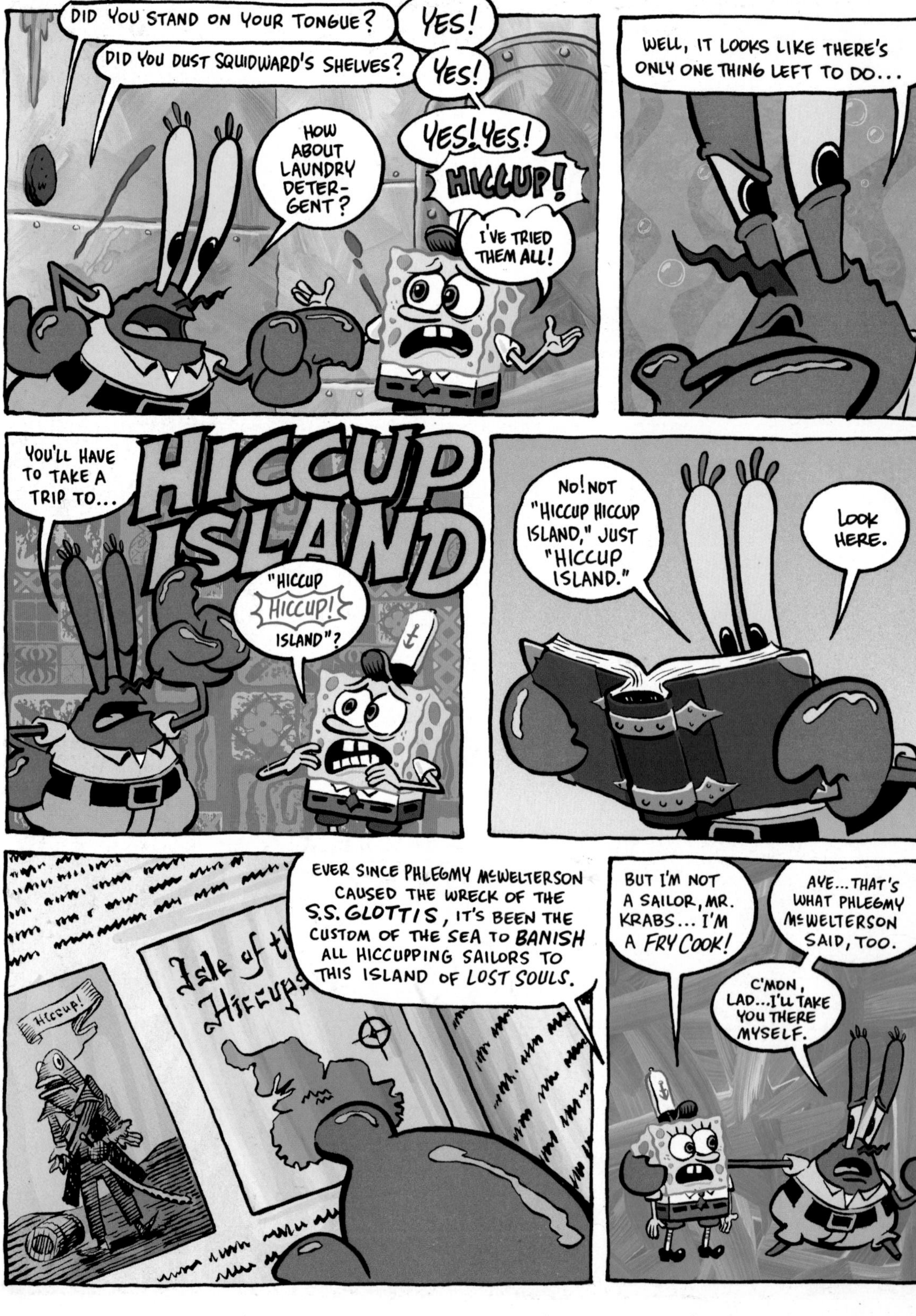
DID YOU STAND ON YOUR TONGUE?
YES!
DID YOU DUST SQUIDWARD'S SHELVES?
YES!
HOW ABOUT LAUNDRY DETER-GENT?
YES! YES!
HICCUP!
I'VE TRIED THEM ALL!
WELL, IT LOOKS LIKE THERE'S ONLY ONE THING LEFT TO DO...
YOU'LL HAVE TO TAKE A TRIP TO...
HICCUP ISLAND
"HICCUP HICCUP! ISLAND"?
NO! NOT "HICCUP HICCUP ISLAND," JUST "HICCUP ISLAND."
LOOK HERE.
EVER SINCE PHLEGMY McWELTERSON CAUSED THE WRECK OF THE S.S. GLOTTIS, IT'S BEEN THE CUSTOM OF THE SEA TO BANISH ALL HICCUPPING SAILORS TO THIS ISLAND OF LOST SOULS.
Isle of the Hiccups
HICCUP!
BUT I'M NOT A SAILOR, MR. KRABS... I'M A FRY COOK!
AYE... THAT'S WHAT PHLEGMY McWELTERSON SAID, TOO.
C'MON, LAD... I'LL TAKE YOU THERE MYSELF.

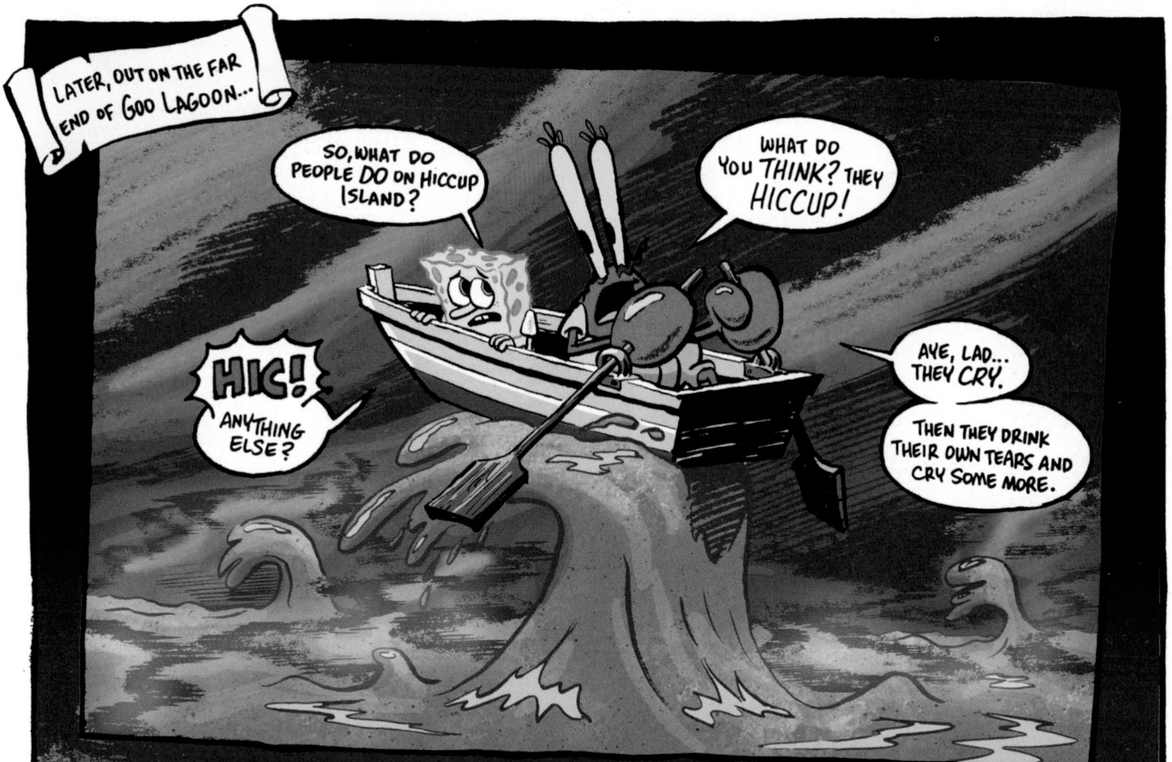
LATER, OUT ON THE FAR END OF GOO LAGOON...
SO, WHAT DO PEOPLE DO ON HICCUP ISLAND?
WHAT DO YOU THINK? THEY HICCUP!
HIC! ANYTHING ELSE?
AYE, LAD... THEY CRY.
THEN THEY DRINK THEIR OWN TEARS AND CRY SOME MORE.

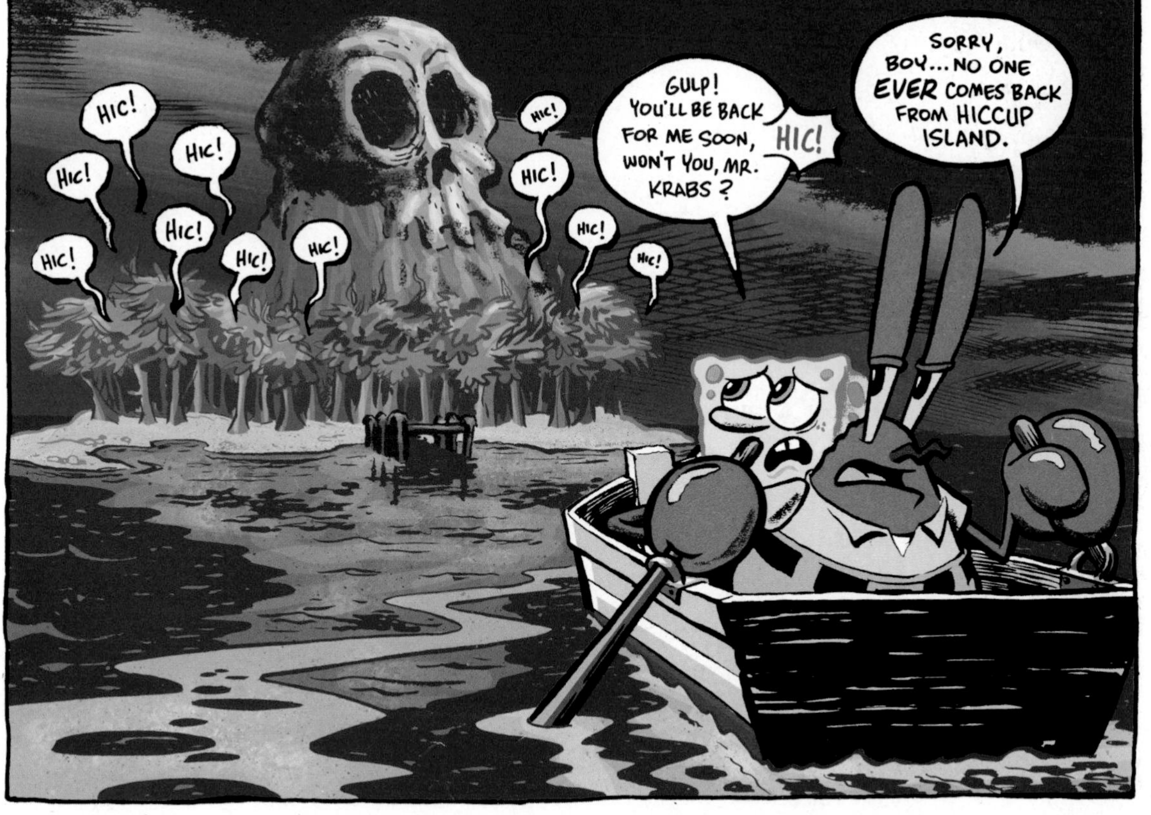
HIC!
HIC!
HIC!
HIC!
HIC!
HIC!
HIC!
HIC!
HIC!
HIC!
HIC!
GULP! YOU'LL BE BACK FOR ME SOON, WON'T YOU, MR. KRABS? HIC!
SORRY, BOY... NO ONE EVER COMES BACK FROM HICCUP ISLAND.

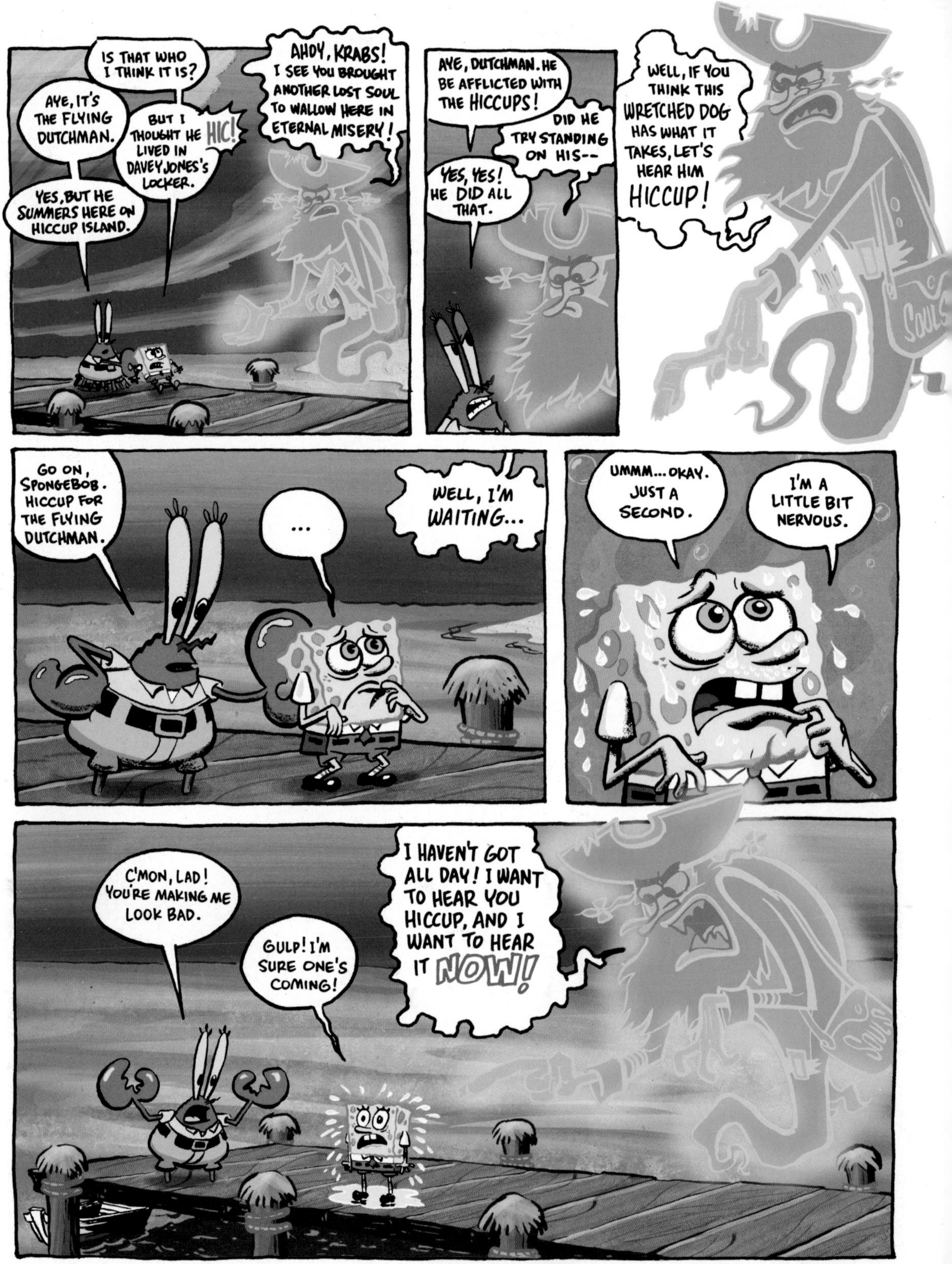

IS THAT WHO I THINK IT IS?
AYE, IT'S THE FLYING DUTCHMAN.
BUT I THOUGHT HE HIC! LIVED IN DAVEY JONES'S LOCKER.
YES, BUT HE SUMMERS HERE ON HICCUP ISLAND.
AHOY, KRABS! I SEE YOU BROUGHT ANOTHER LOST SOUL TO WALLOW HERE IN ETERNAL MISERY!
AYE, DUTCHMAN. HE BE AFFLICTED WITH THE HICCUPS!
DID HE TRY STANDING ON HIS--
YES, YES! HE DID ALL THAT.
WELL, IF YOU THINK THIS WRETCHED DOG HAS WHAT IT TAKES, LET'S HEAR HIM HICCUP!
SOULS
GO ON, SPONGEBOB. HICCUP FOR THE FLYING DUTCHMAN.
...
WELL, I'M WAITING...
UMMM... OKAY. JUST A SECOND.
I'M A LITTLE BIT NERVOUS.
C'MON, LAD! YOU'RE MAKING ME LOOK BAD.
GULP! I'M SURE ONE'S COMING!
I HAVEN'T GOT ALL DAY! I WANT TO HEAR YOU HICCUP, AND I WANT TO HEAR IT NOW!
SOULS

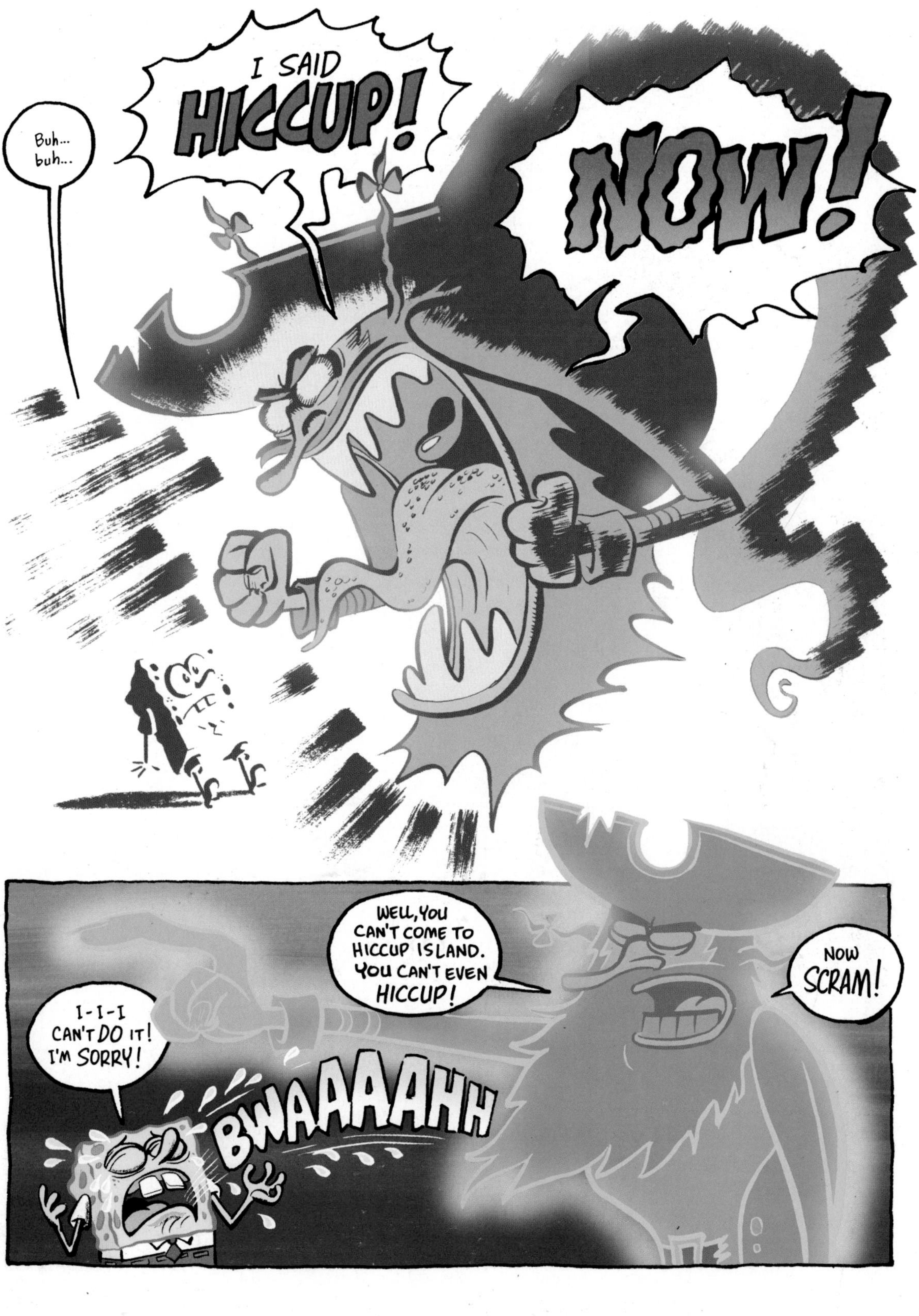
Buh... buh...
I SAID HICCUP!
NOW!
WELL, YOU CAN'T COME TO HICCUP ISLAND. YOU CAN'T EVEN HICCUP!
NOW SCRAM!
I-I-I CAN'T DO IT! I'M SORRY!
BWAAAAAHH

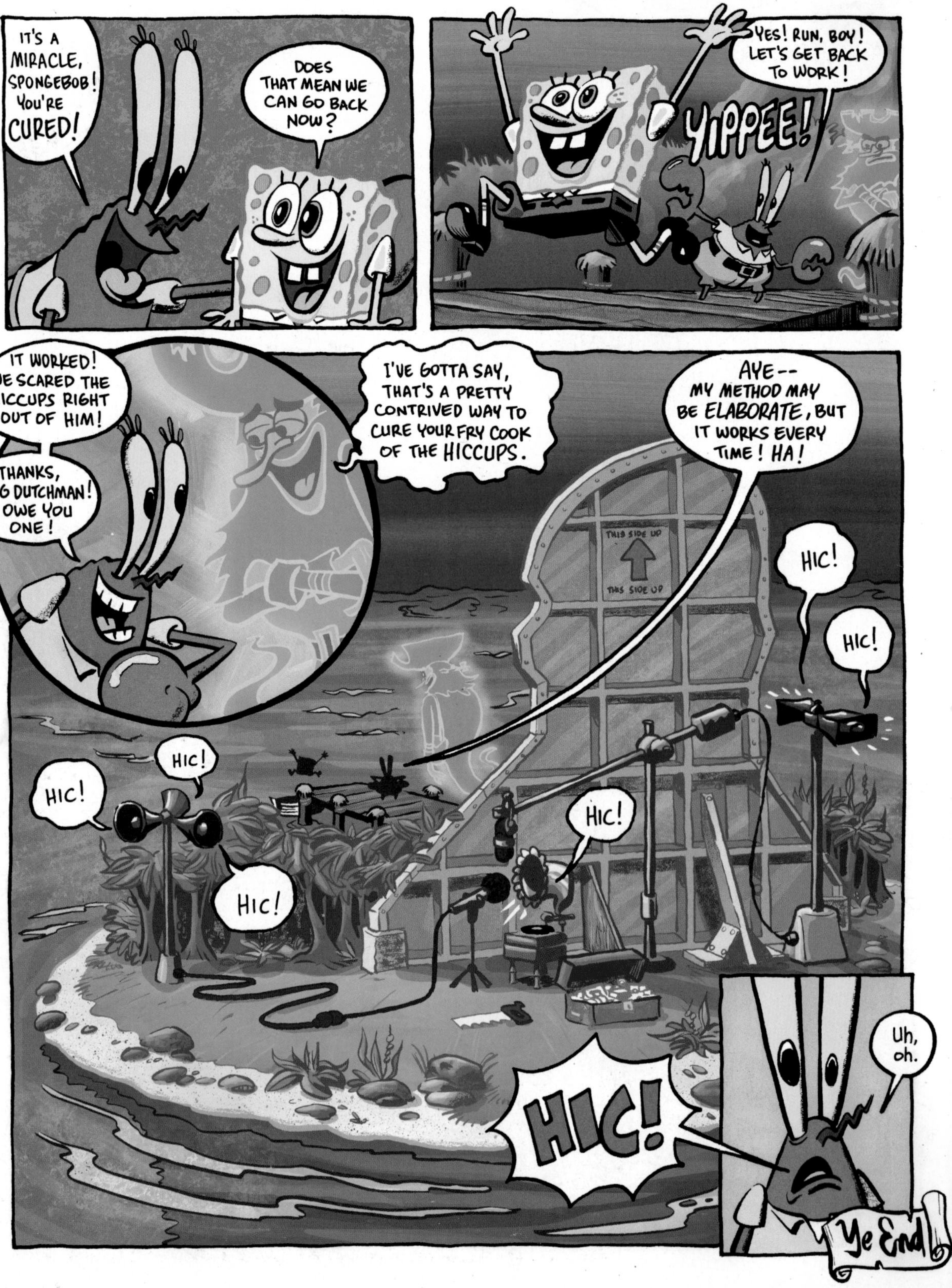

IT'S A MIRACLE, SPONGEBOB! YOU'RE CURED!
DOES THAT MEAN WE CAN GO BACK NOW?
YIPPEE!
YES! RUN, BOY! LET'S GET BACK TO WORK!
IT WORKED! WE SCARED THE HICCUPS RIGHT OUT OF HIM!
THANKS, FLYING DUTCHMAN! I OWE YOU ONE!
I'VE GOTTA SAY, THAT'S A PRETTY CONTRIVED WAY TO CURE YOUR FRY COOK OF THE HICCUPS.
AYE-- MY METHOD MAY BE ELABORATE, BUT IT WORKS EVERY TIME! HA!
THIS SIDE UP
THIS SIDE UP
HIC!
HIC!
HIC!
HIC!
HIC!
HIC!
HIC!
Uh, oh.
Ye End

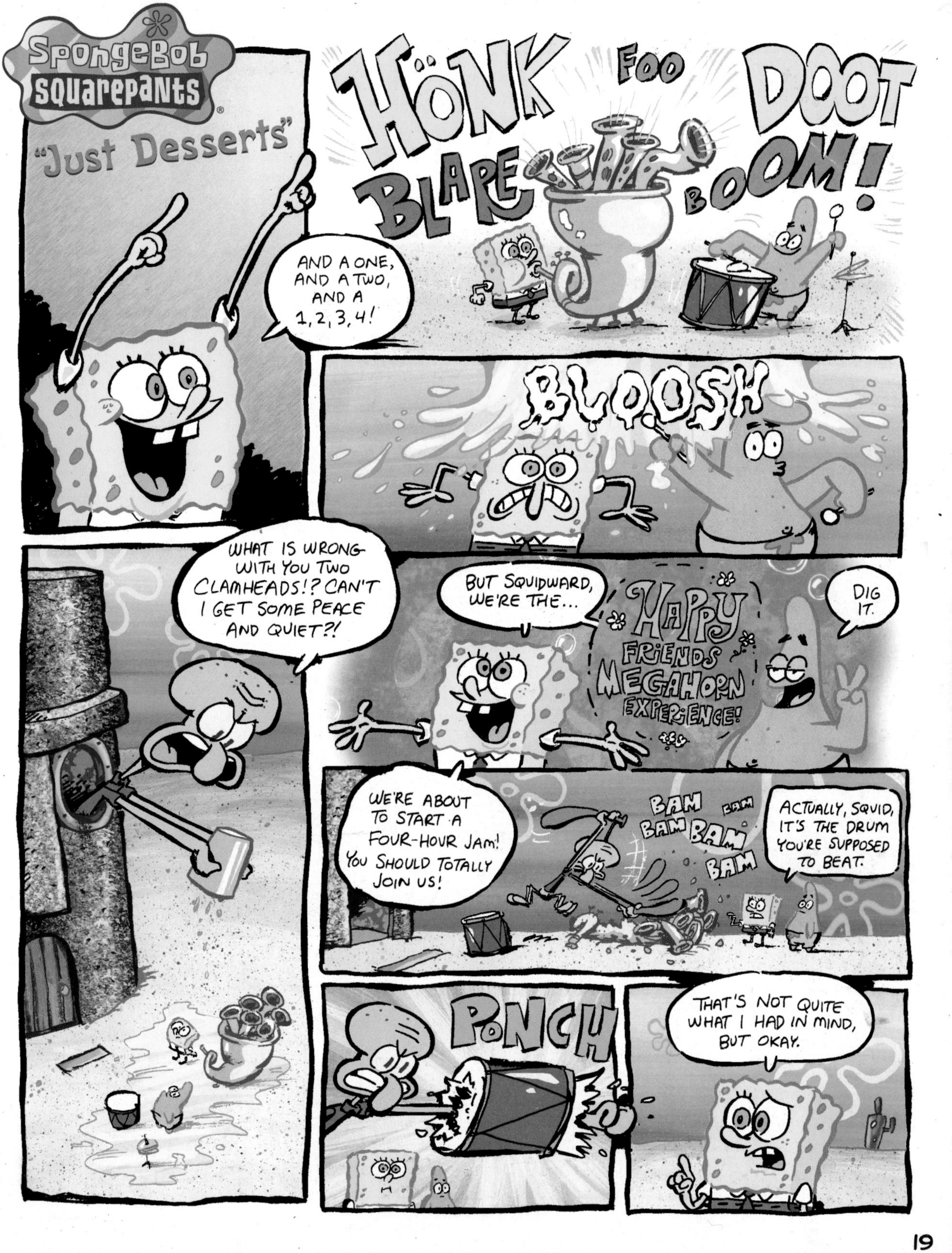

SpongeBob SquarePants
"Just Desserts"
AND A ONE, AND A TWO, AND A 1, 2, 3, 4!
HONK FOO DOOT BLAPE BOOM!
BLOOSH
WHAT IS WRONG WITH YOU TWO CLAMHEADS!? CAN'T I GET SOME PEACE AND QUIET?!
BUT SQUIDWARD, WE'RE THE...
HAPPY FRIENDS MEGAHORN EXPERIENCE!
DIG IT.
WE'RE ABOUT TO START A FOUR-HOUR JAM! YOU SHOULD TOTALLY JOIN US!
BAM BAM BAM BAM BAM BAM
ACTUALLY, SQUID, IT'S THE DRUM YOU'RE SUPPOSED TO BEAT.
PONCH
THAT'S NOT QUITE WHAT I HAD IN MIND, BUT OKAY.

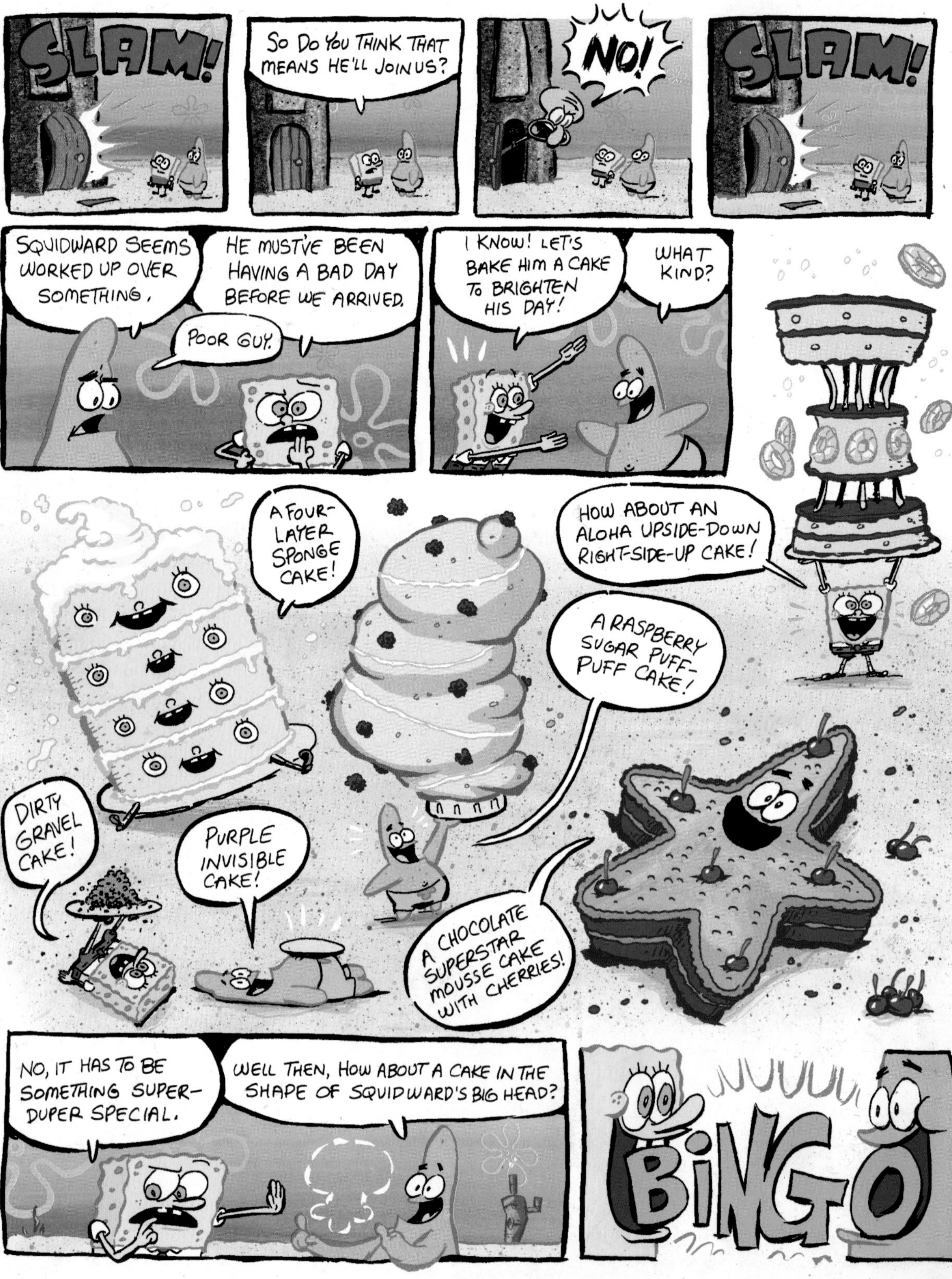
SLAM!
SO DO YOU THINK THAT MEANS HE'LL JOIN US?
NO!
SLAM!
SQUIDWARD SEEMS WORKED UP OVER SOMETHING.
HE MUST'VE BEEN HAVING A BAD DAY BEFORE WE ARRIVED.
POOR GUY.
I KNOW! LET'S BAKE HIM A CAKE TO BRIGHTEN HIS DAY!
WHAT KIND?
A FOUR-LAYER SPONGE CAKE!
HOW ABOUT AN ALOHA UPSIDE-DOWN RIGHT-SIDE-UP CAKE!
A RASPBERRY SUGAR PUFF-PUFF CAKE!
DIRTY GRAVEL CAKE!
PURPLE INVISIBLE CAKE!
A CHOCOLATE SUPERSTAR MOUSSE CAKE WITH CHERRIES!
NO, IT HAS TO BE SOMETHING SUPER-DUPER SPECIAL.
WELL THEN, HOW ABOUT A CAKE IN THE SHAPE OF SQUIDWARD'S BIG HEAD?
BINGO

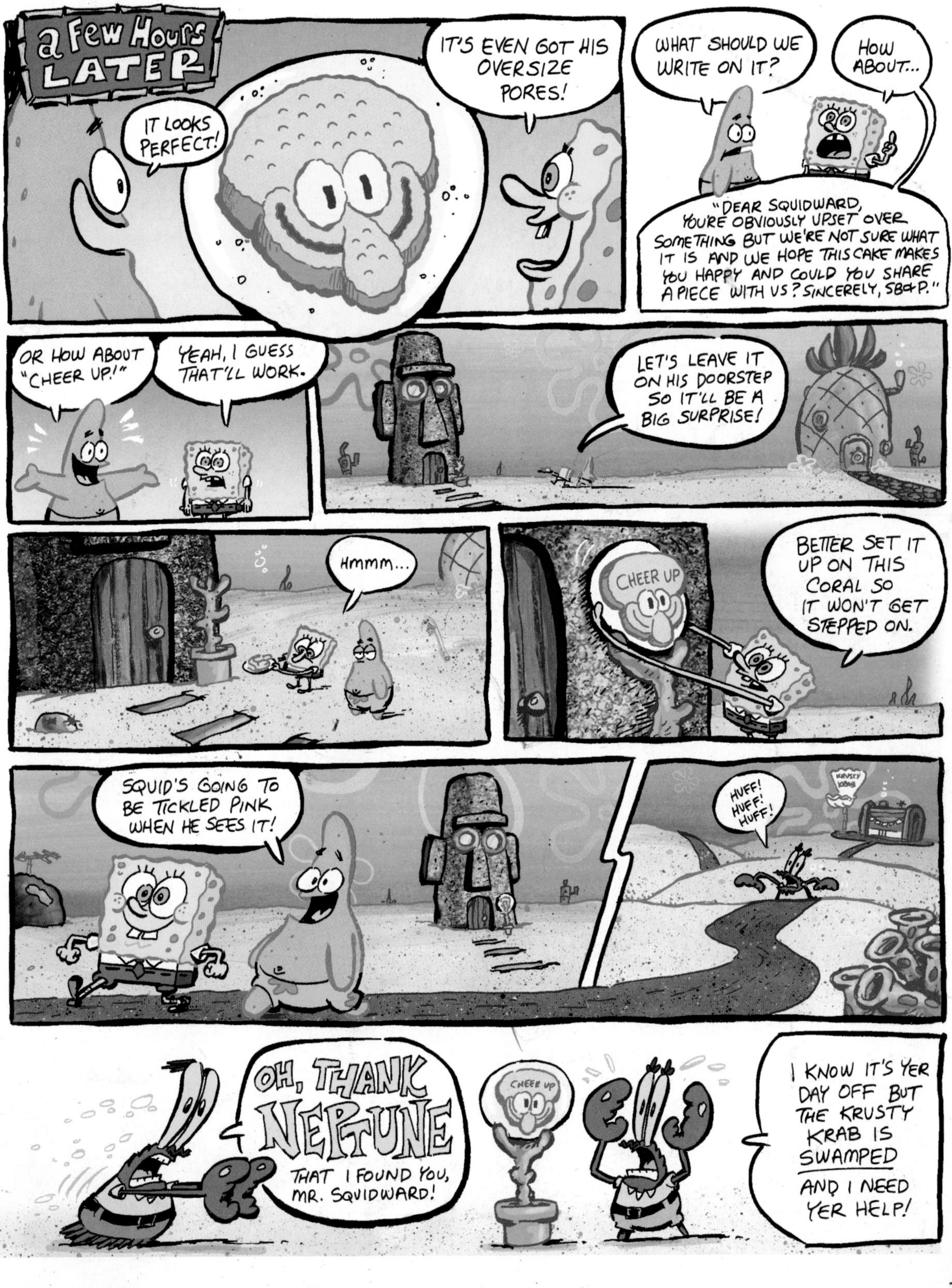
a Few Hours LATER
IT LOOKS PERFECT!
IT'S EVEN GOT HIS OVERSIZE PORES!
WHAT SHOULD WE WRITE ON IT?
HOW ABOUT...
"DEAR SQUIDWARD, YOU'RE OBVIOUSLY UPSET OVER SOMETHING BUT WE'RE NOT SURE WHAT IT IS AND WE HOPE THIS CAKE MAKES YOU HAPPY AND COULD YOU SHARE A PIECE WITH US? SINCERELY, SB&P."
OR HOW ABOUT "CHEER UP!"
YEAH, I GUESS THAT'LL WORK.
LET'S LEAVE IT ON HIS DOORSTEP SO IT'LL BE A BIG SURPRISE!
Hmmm...
CHEER UP
BETTER SET IT UP ON THIS CORAL SO IT WON'T GET STEPPED ON.
SQUID'S GOING TO BE TICKLED PINK WHEN HE SEES IT!
HUFF! HUFF! HUFF!
OH, THANK NEPTUNE THAT I FOUND YOU, MR. SQUIDWARD!
CHEER UP
I KNOW IT'S YER DAY OFF BUT THE KRUSTY KRAB IS SWAMPED AND I NEED YER HELP!

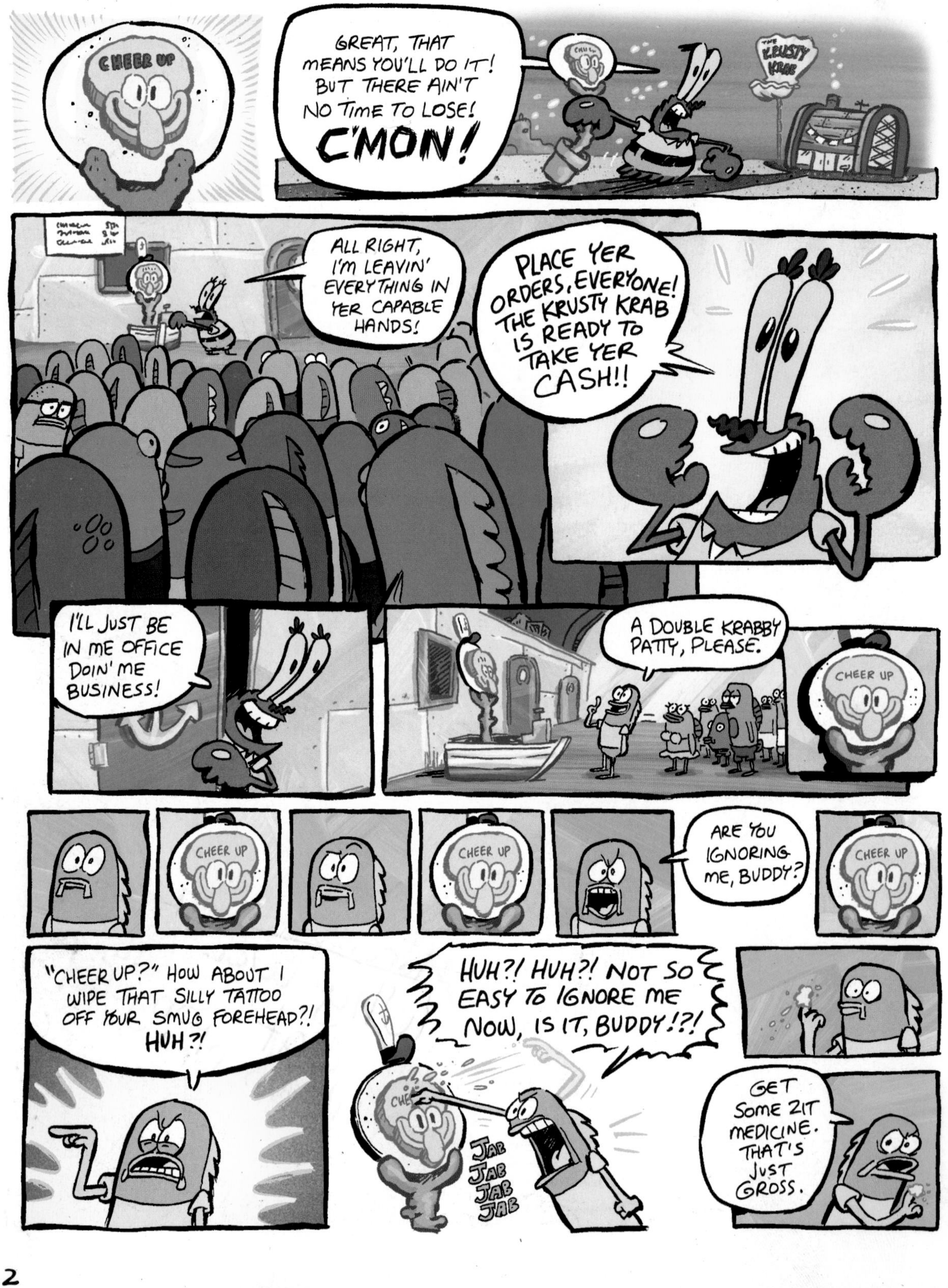

CHEER UP
GREAT, THAT MEANS YOU'LL DO IT! BUT THERE AIN'T NO TIME TO LOSE! C'MON!
THE KRUSTY KRAB
ALL RIGHT, I'M LEAVIN' EVERYTHING IN YER CAPABLE HANDS!
PLACE YER ORDERS, EVERYONE! THE KRUSTY KRAB IS READY TO TAKE YER CASH!!
I'LL JUST BE IN ME OFFICE DOIN' ME BUSINESS!
A DOUBLE KRABBY PATTY, PLEASE.
CHEER UP
CHEER UP
CHEER UP
ARE YOU IGNORING ME, BUDDY?
CHEER UP
"CHEER UP?" HOW ABOUT I WIPE THAT SILLY TATTOO OFF YOUR SMUG FOREHEAD?! HUH?!
HUH?! HUH?! NOT SO EASY TO IGNORE ME NOW, IS IT, BUDDY!?!
JAB JAB JAB JAB
GET SOME ZIT MEDICINE. THAT'S JUST GROSS.

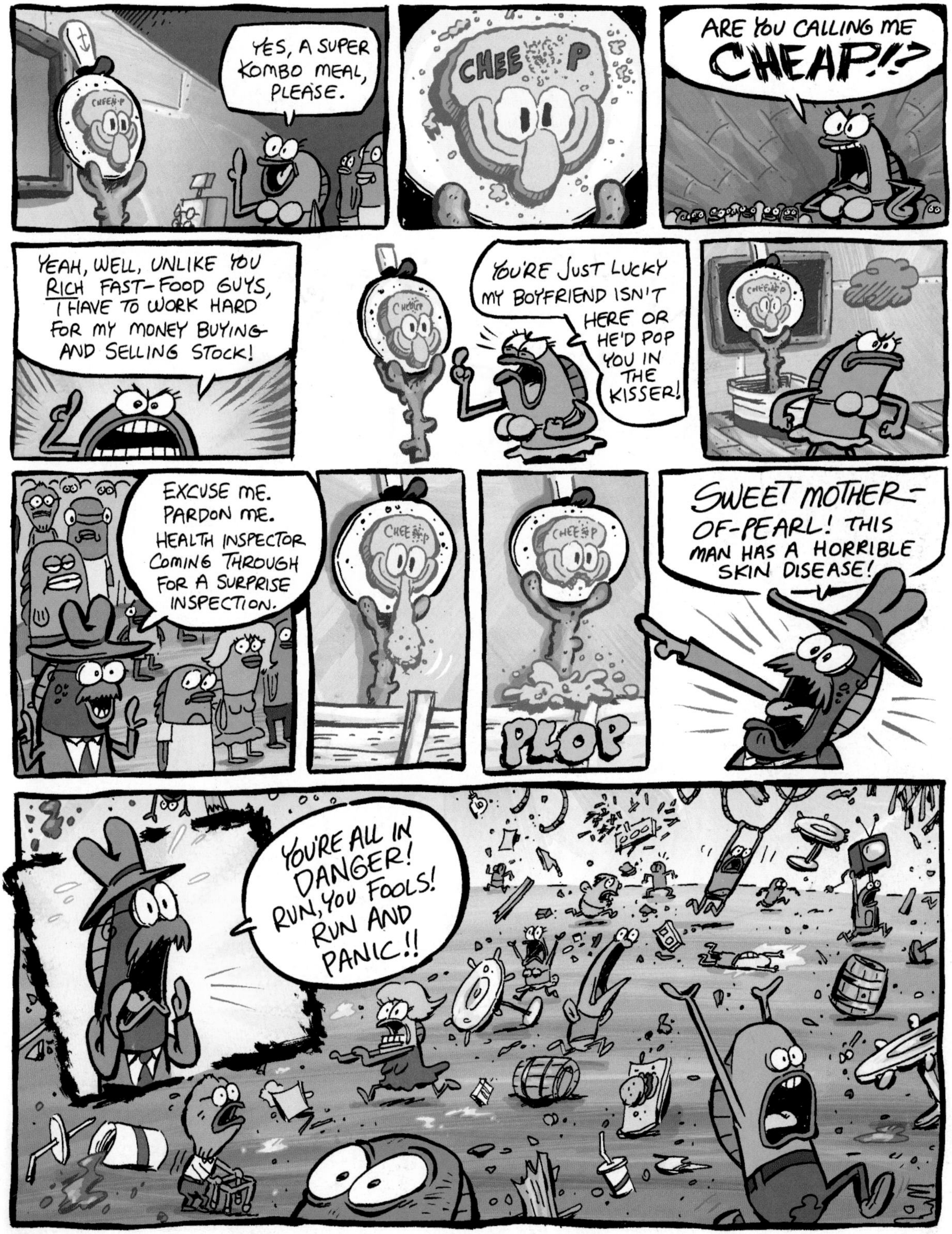
YES, A SUPER KOMBO MEAL, PLEASE.
CHEE P
ARE YOU CALLING ME CHEAP!?
YEAH, WELL, UNLIKE YOU RICH FAST-FOOD GUYS, I HAVE TO WORK HARD FOR MY MONEY BUYING AND SELLING STOCK!
YOU'RE JUST LUCKY MY BOYFRIEND ISN'T HERE OR HE'D POP YOU IN THE KISSER!
EXCUSE ME. PARDON ME. HEALTH INSPECTOR COMING THROUGH FOR A SURPRISE INSPECTION.
PLOP
SWEET MOTHER-OF-PEARL! THIS MAN HAS A HORRIBLE SKIN DISEASE!
YOU'RE ALL IN DANGER! RUN, YOU FOOLS! RUN AND PANIC!!

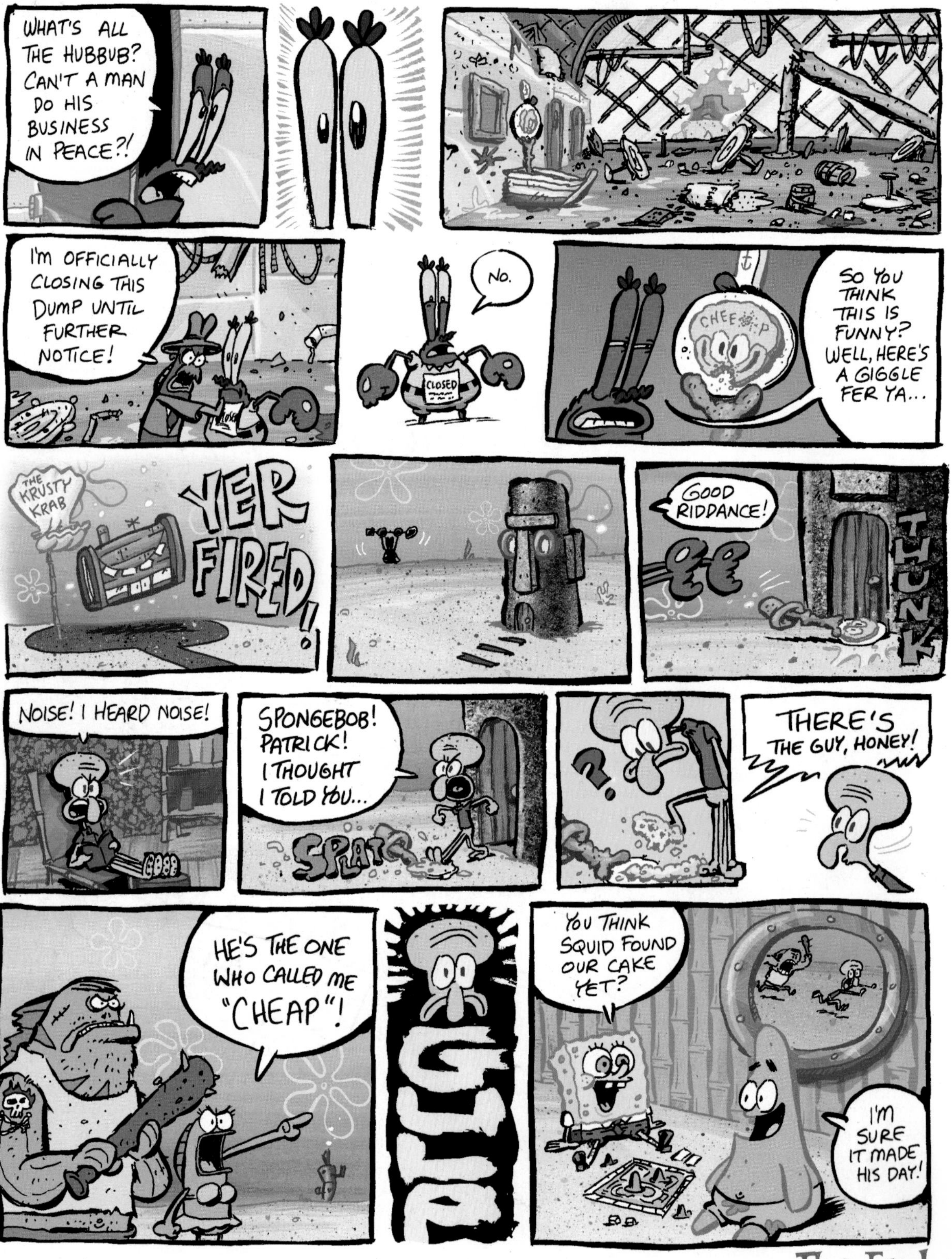
WHAT'S ALL THE HUBBUB? CAN'T A MAN DO HIS BUSINESS IN PEACE?!
I'M OFFICIALLY CLOSING THIS DUMP UNTIL FURTHER NOTICE!
CLOSED
NO.
SO YOU THINK THIS IS FUNNY? WELL, HERE'S A GIGGLE FER YA...
THE KRUSTY KRAB
YER FIRED!
GOOD RIDDANCE!
THUNK
NOISE! I HEARD NOISE!
SPONGEBOB! PATRICK! I THOUGHT I TOLD YOU...
SPLAT
THERE'S THE GUY, HONEY!
HE'S THE ONE WHO CALLED ME "CHEAP"!
GULP
YOU THINK SQUID FOUND OUR CAKE YET?
I'M SURE IT MADE HIS DAY!

The End

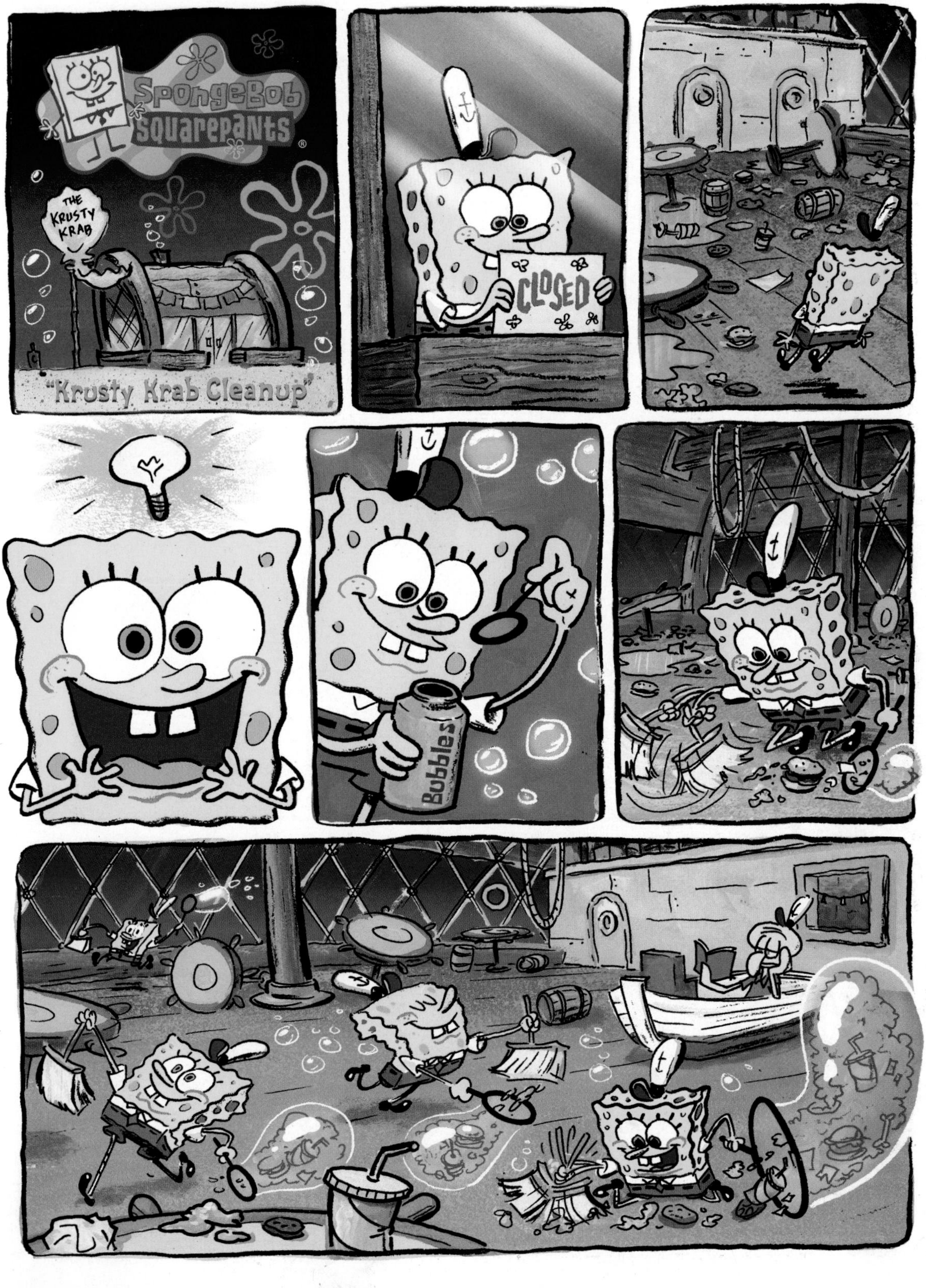
SpongeBob SquarePants®
THE KRUSTY KRAB
"Krusty Krab Cleanup"
CLOSED
Bubbles

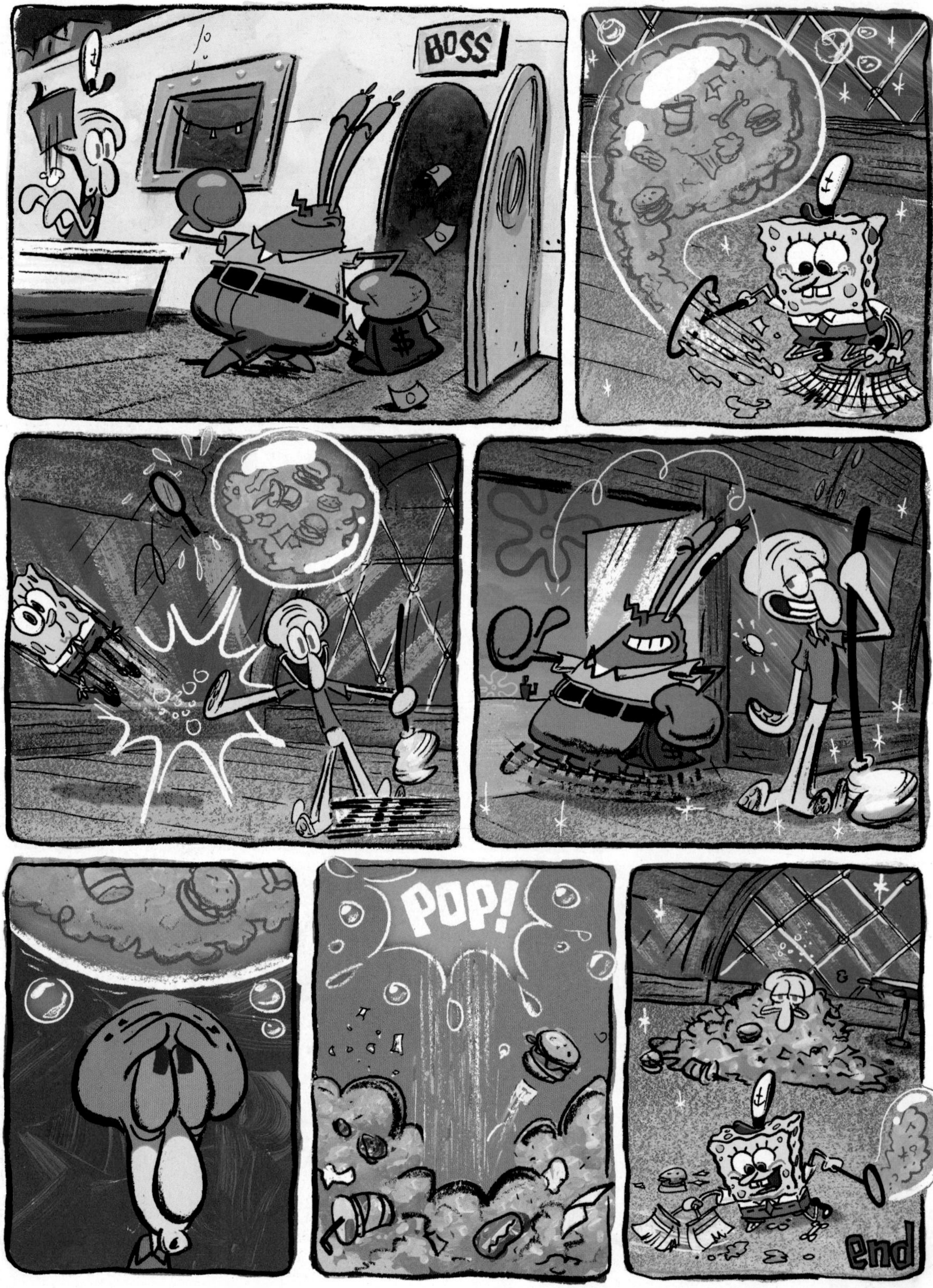
BOSS
POP!
end

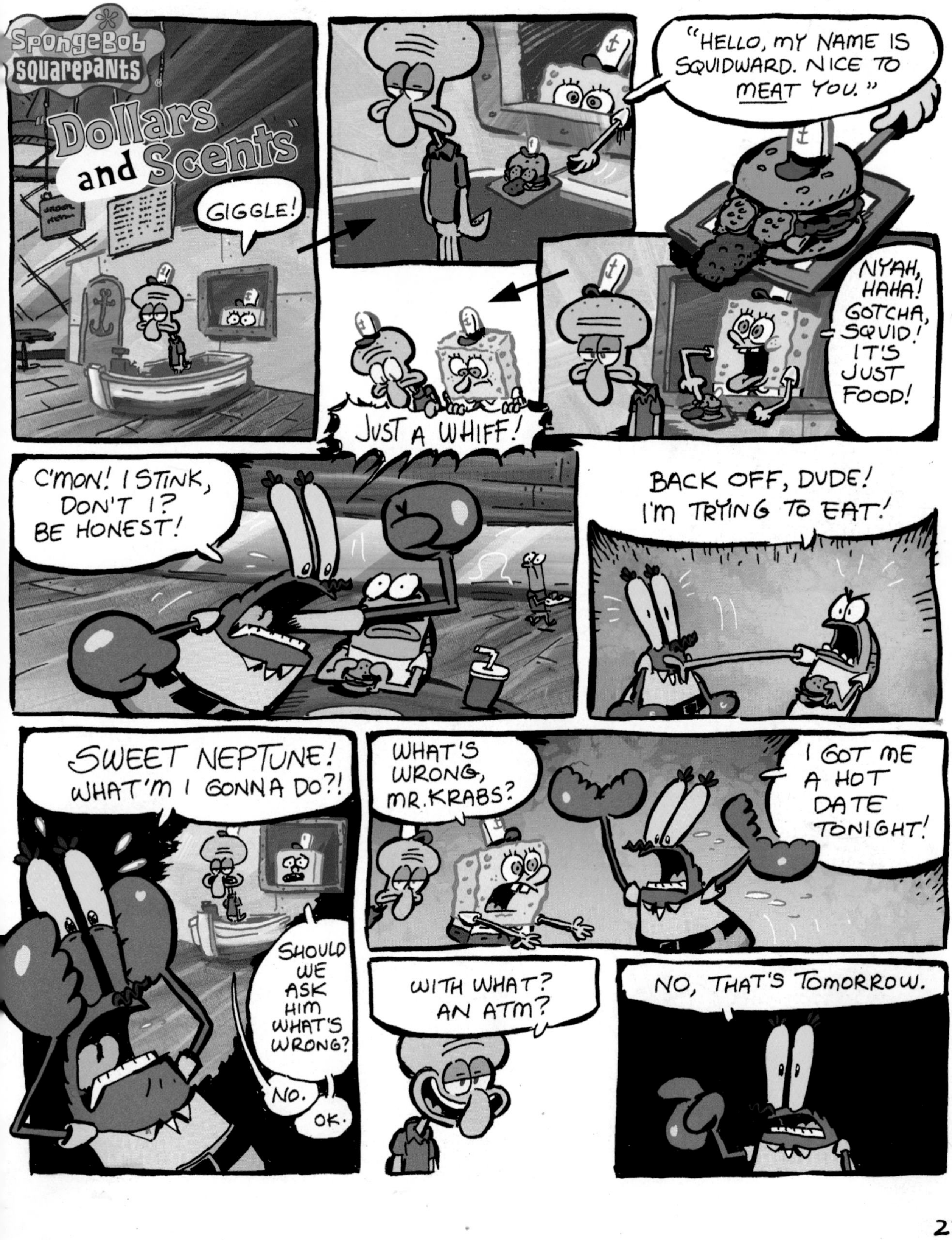
SpongeBob SquarePants
"Dollars and Scents"
GIGGLE!
"HELLO, MY NAME IS SQUIDWARD. NICE TO MEAT YOU."
NYAH, HAHA! GOTCHA, SQUID! IT'S JUST FOOD!
JUST A WHIFF!
C'MON! I STINK, DON'T I? BE HONEST!
BACK OFF, DUDE! I'M TRYING TO EAT!
SWEET NEPTUNE! WHAT'M I GONNA DO?!
SHOULD WE ASK HIM WHAT'S WRONG?
NO.
OK.
WHAT'S WRONG, MR. KRABS?
I GOT ME A HOT DATE TONIGHT!
WITH WHAT? AN ATM?
NO, THAT'S TOMORROW.

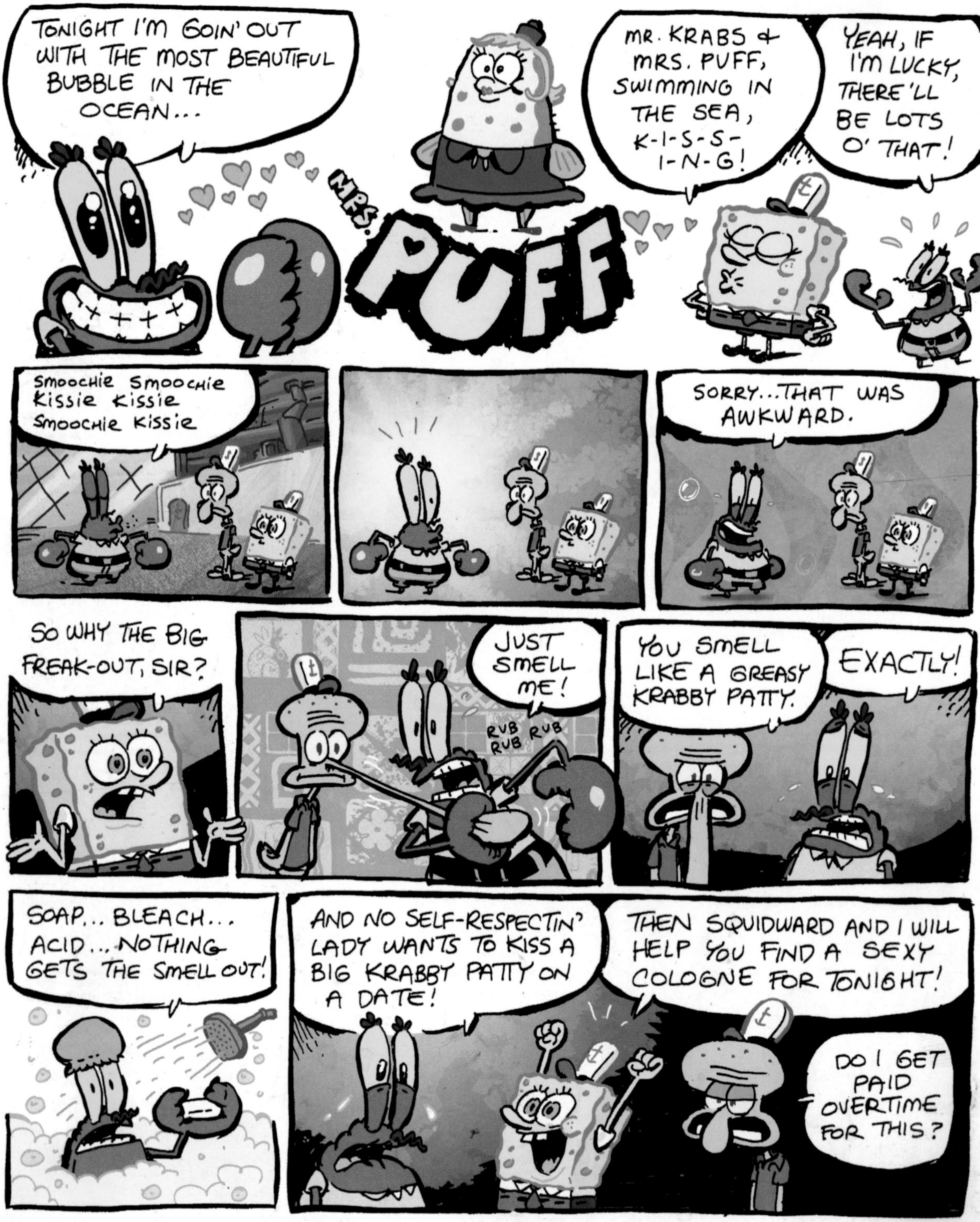
TONIGHT I'M GOIN' OUT WITH THE MOST BEAUTIFUL BUBBLE IN THE OCEAN...
MRS. PUFF
MR. KRABS & MRS. PUFF, SWIMMING IN THE SEA, K-I-S-S-I-N-G!
YEAH, IF I'M LUCKY, THERE'LL BE LOTS O' THAT!
SMOOCHIE SMOOCHIE KISSIE KISSIE SMOOCHIE KISSIE
SORRY...THAT WAS AWKWARD.
SO WHY THE BIG FREAK-OUT, SIR?
JUST SMELL ME!
RUB RUB RUB RUB
YOU SMELL LIKE A GREASY KRABBY PATTY.
EXACTLY!
SOAP... BLEACH... ACID... NOTHING GETS THE SMELL OUT!
AND NO SELF-RESPECTIN' LADY WANTS TO KISS A BIG KRABBY PATTY ON A DATE!
THEN SQUIDWARD AND I WILL HELP YOU FIND A SEXY COLOGNE FOR TONIGHT!
DO I GET PAID OVERTIME FOR THIS?

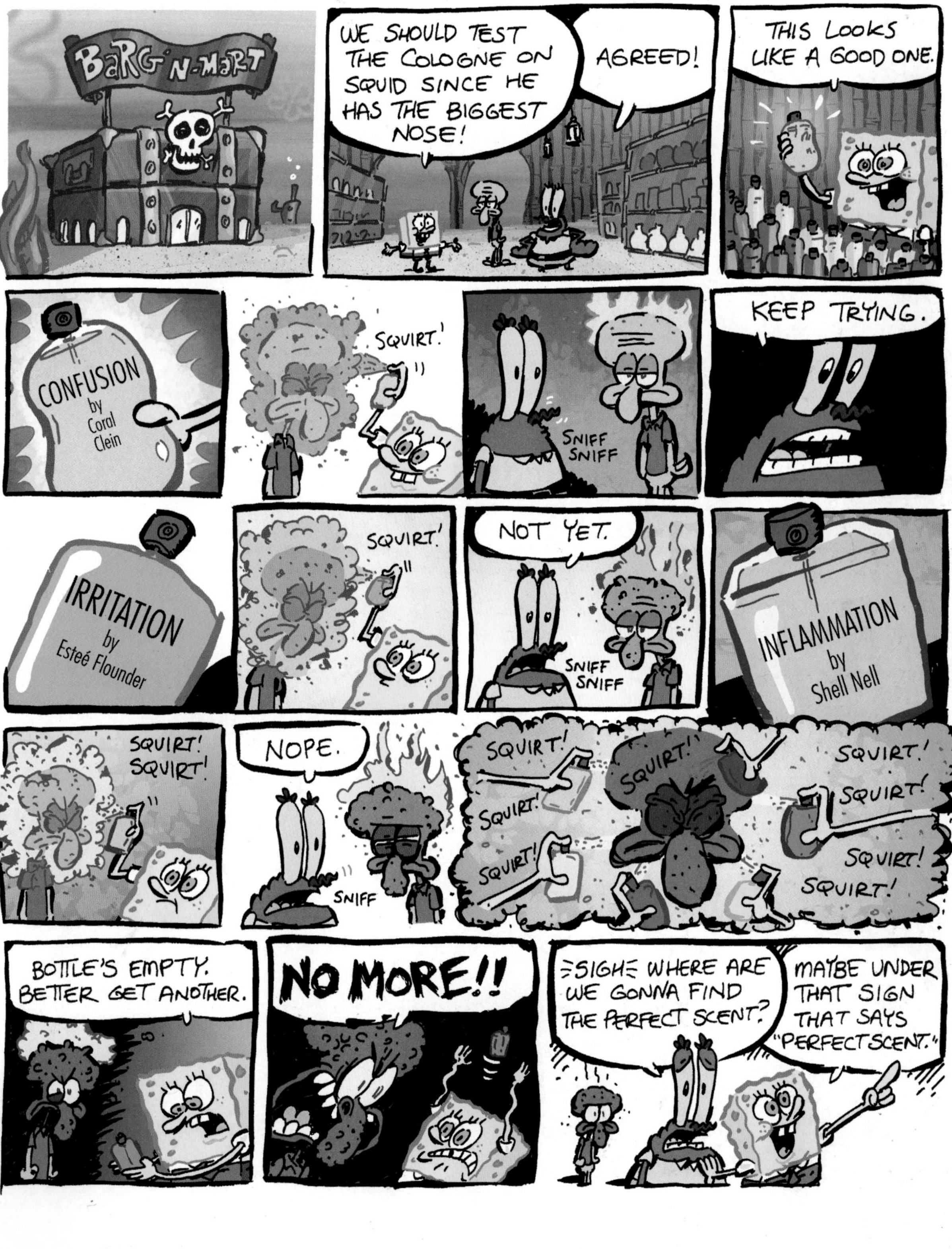

BARG'N-MART
WE SHOULD TEST THE COLOGNE ON SQUID SINCE HE HAS THE BIGGEST NOSE!
AGREED!
THIS LOOKS LIKE A GOOD ONE.
CONFUSION by Coral Clein
SQUIRT!
SNIFF SNIFF
KEEP TRYING.
IRRITATION by Esteé Flounder
SQUIRT!
NOT YET.
SNIFF SNIFF
INFLAMMATION by Shell Nell
SQUIRT! SQUIRT!
NOPE.
SNIFF
SQUIRT!
SQUIRT!
SQUIRT!
SQUIRT!
SQUIRT!
SQUIRT!
SQUIRT!
SQUIRT!
BOTTLE'S EMPTY. BETTER GET ANOTHER.
NO MORE!!
SIGH WHERE ARE WE GONNA FIND THE PERFECT SCENT?
MAYBE UNDER THAT SIGN THAT SAYS "PERFECT SCENT."

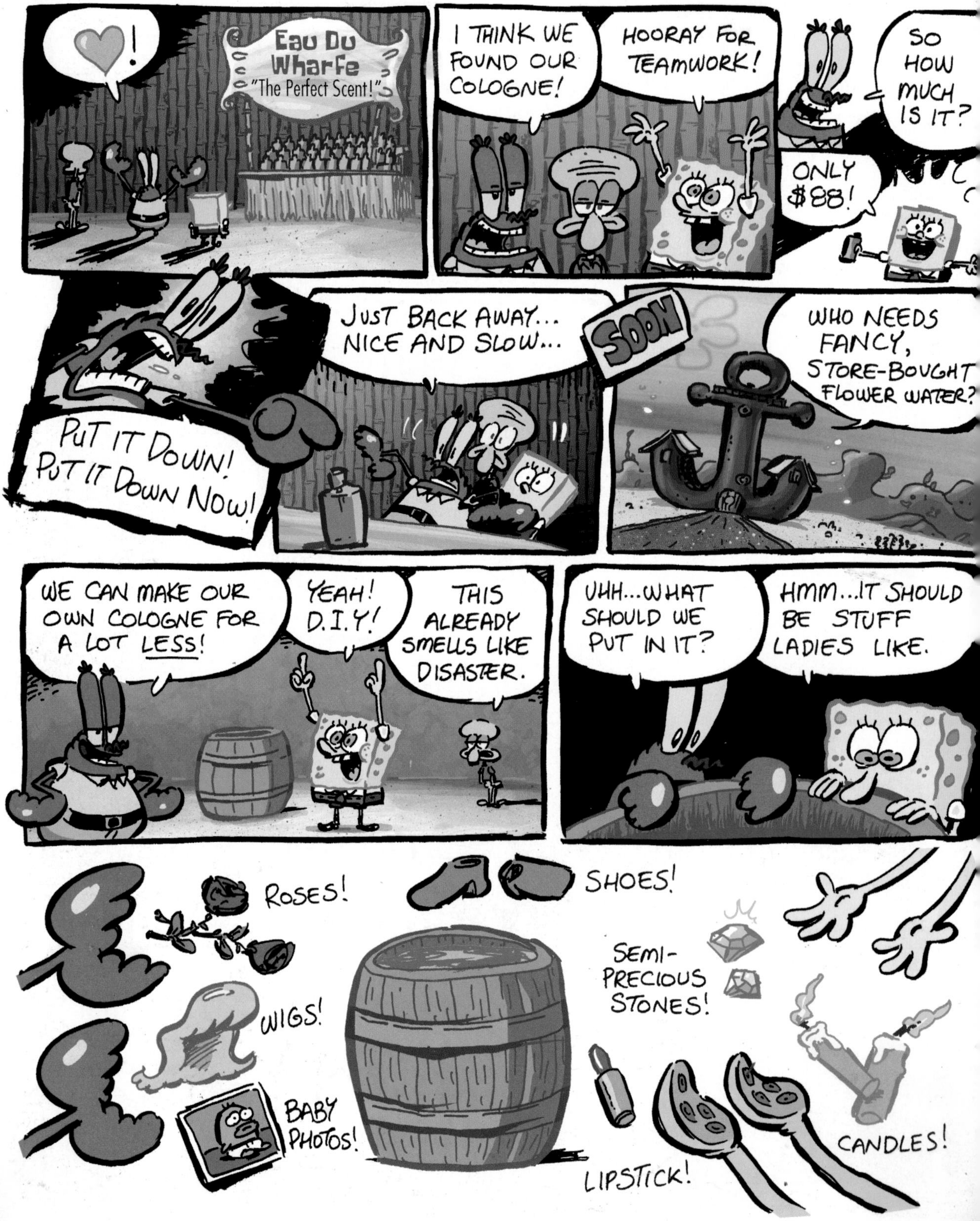
Eau Du Wharfe
"The Perfect Scent!"
I THINK WE FOUND OUR COLOGNE!
HOORAY FOR TEAMWORK!
SO HOW MUCH IS IT?
ONLY $88!
JUST BACK AWAY... NICE AND SLOW...
PUT IT DOWN! PUT IT DOWN NOW!
SOON
WHO NEEDS FANCY, STORE-BOUGHT FLOWER WATER?
WE CAN MAKE OUR OWN COLOGNE FOR A LOT LESS!
YEAH! D.I.Y!
THIS ALREADY SMELLS LIKE DISASTER.
UHH...WHAT SHOULD WE PUT IN IT?
HMM...IT SHOULD BE STUFF LADIES LIKE.
ROSES!
SHOES!
WIGS!
SEMI-PRECIOUS STONES!
BABY PHOTOS!
LIPSTICK!
CANDLES!

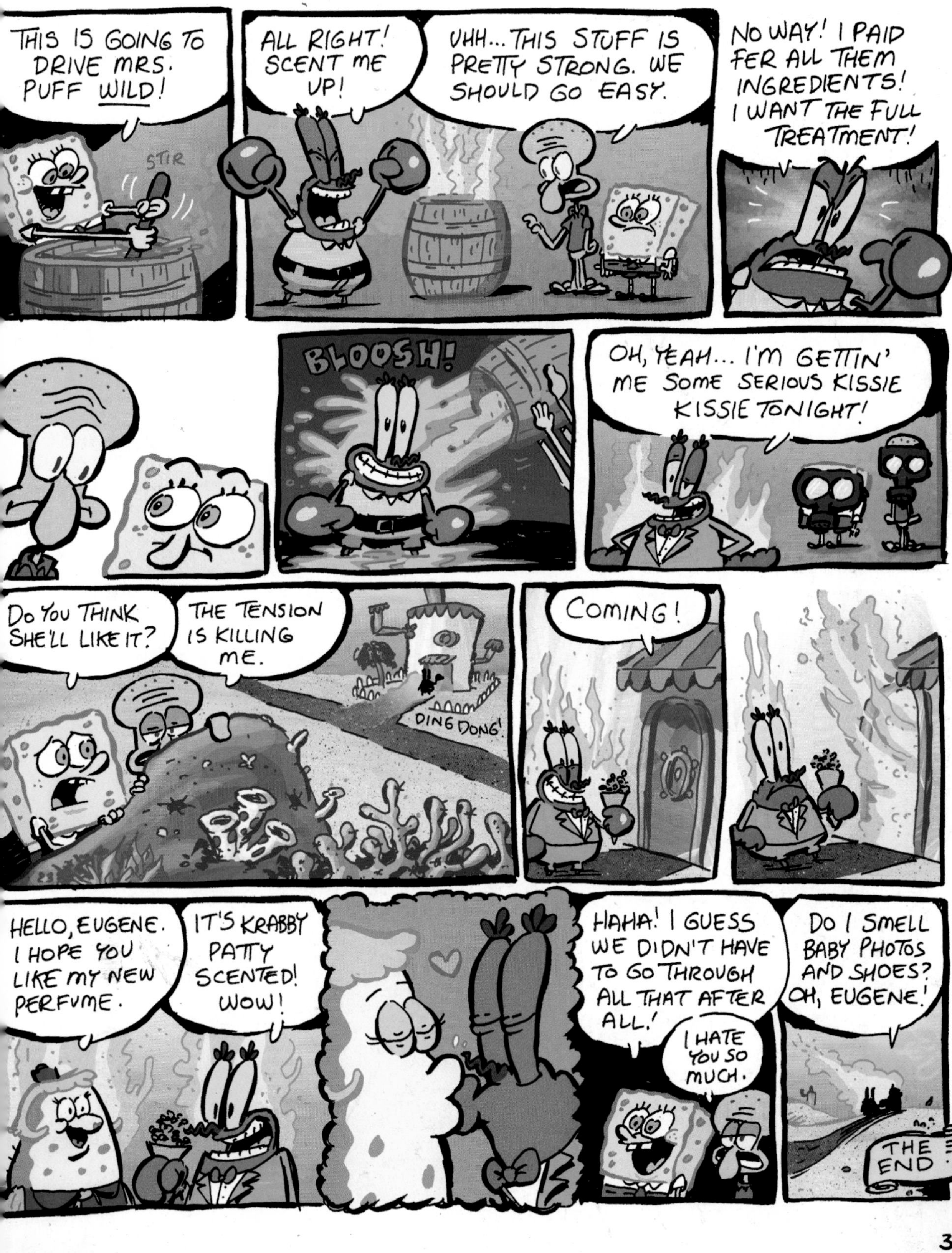
THIS IS GOING TO DRIVE MRS. PUFF WILD!
STIR
ALL RIGHT! SCENT ME UP!
UHH... THIS STUFF IS PRETTY STRONG. WE SHOULD GO EASY.
NO WAY! I PAID FER ALL THEM INGREDIENTS! I WANT THE FULL TREATMENT!
BLOOSH!
OH, YEAH... I'M GETTIN' ME SOME SERIOUS KISSIE KISSIE TONIGHT!
DO YOU THINK SHE'LL LIKE IT?
THE TENSION IS KILLING ME.
DING DONG!
COMING!
HELLO, EUGENE. I HOPE YOU LIKE MY NEW PERFUME.
IT'S KRABBY PATTY SCENTED! WOW!
HAHA! I GUESS WE DIDN'T HAVE TO GO THROUGH ALL THAT AFTER ALL!
I HATE YOU SO MUCH.
DO I SMELL BABY PHOTOS AND SHOES? OH, EUGENE!
THE END

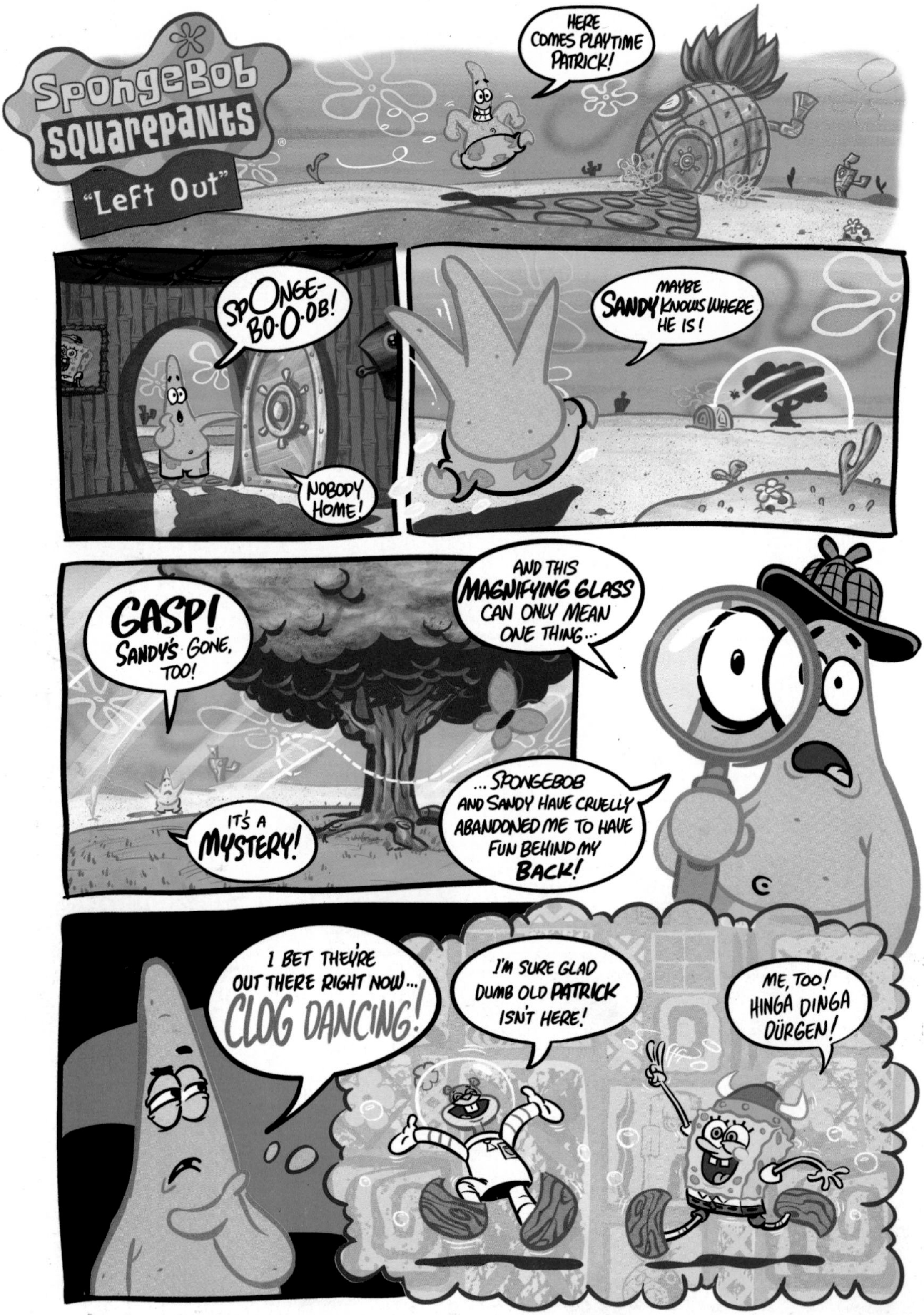
SpongeBob SquarePants
"Left Out"
HERE COMES PLAYTIME PATRICK!
SPONGE-BO-O-OB!
NOBODY HOME!
MAYBE SANDY KNOWS WHERE HE IS!
GASP! SANDY'S GONE, TOO!
AND THIS MAGNIFYING GLASS CAN ONLY MEAN ONE THING...
IT'S A MYSTERY!
...SPONGEBOB AND SANDY HAVE CRUELLY ABANDONED ME TO HAVE FUN BEHIND MY BACK!
I BET THEY'RE OUT THERE RIGHT NOW... CLOG DANCING!
I'M SURE GLAD DUMB OLD PATRICK ISN'T HERE!
ME, TOO! HINGA DINGA DÜRGEN!

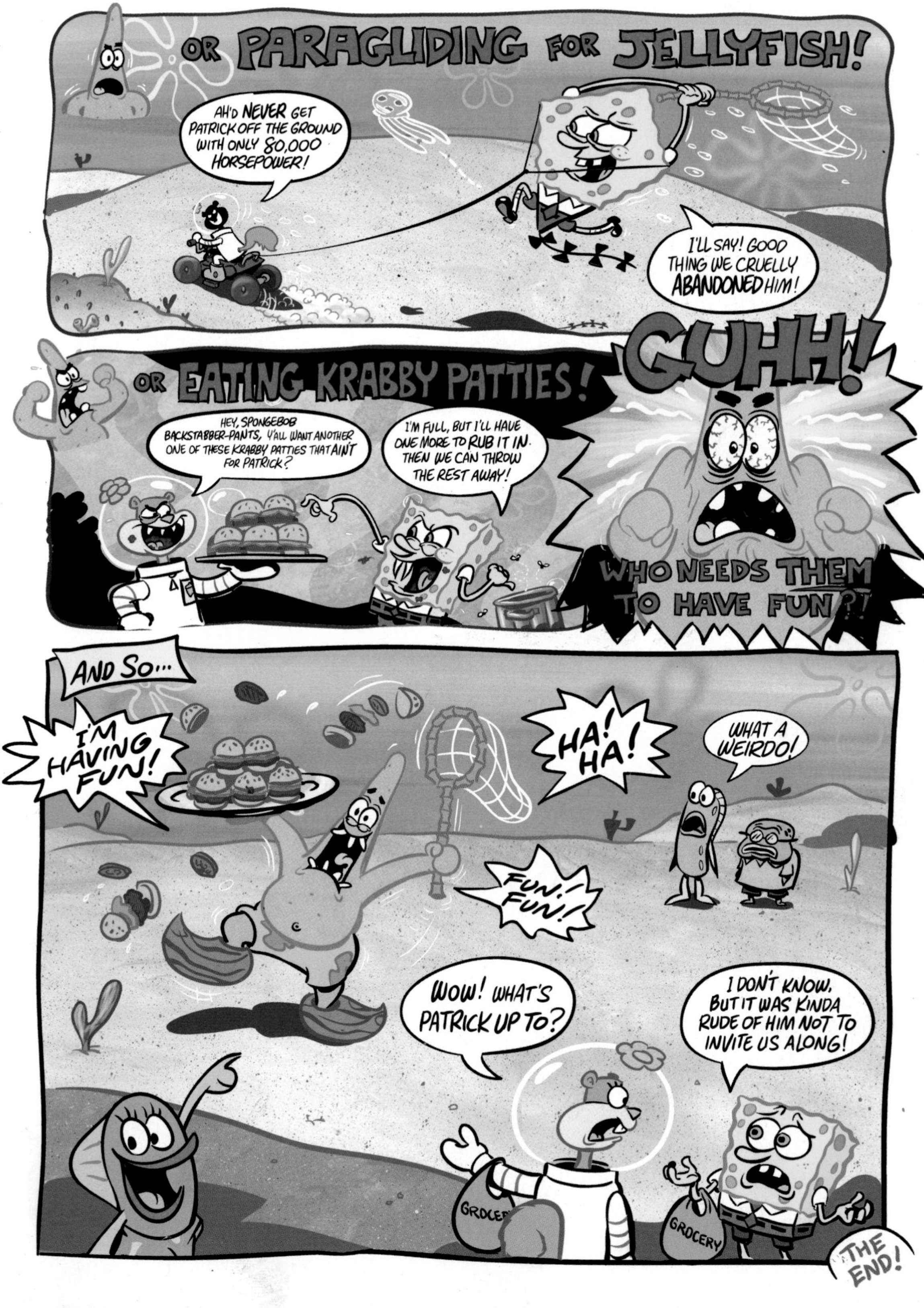
OR PARAGLIDING FOR JELLYFISH!
AH'D NEVER GET PATRICK OFF THE GROUND WITH ONLY 80,000 HORSEPOWER!
I'LL SAY! GOOD THING WE CRUELLY ABANDONED HIM!
OR EATING KRABBY PATTIES!
HEY, SPONGEBOB BACKSTABBER-PANTS, Y'ALL WANT ANOTHER ONE OF THESE KRABBY PATTIES THAT AIN'T FOR PATRICK?
I'M FULL, BUT I'LL HAVE ONE MORE TO RUB IT IN. THEN WE CAN THROW THE REST AWAY!
GUHH!
WHO NEEDS THEM TO HAVE FUN?!
AND SO...
I'M HAVING FUN!
HA! HA!
WHAT A WEIRDO!
FUN! FUN!
WOW! WHAT'S PATRICK UP TO?
I DON'T KNOW. BUT IT WAS KINDA RUDE OF HIM NOT TO INVITE US ALONG!
GROCERY
GROCERY
THE END!

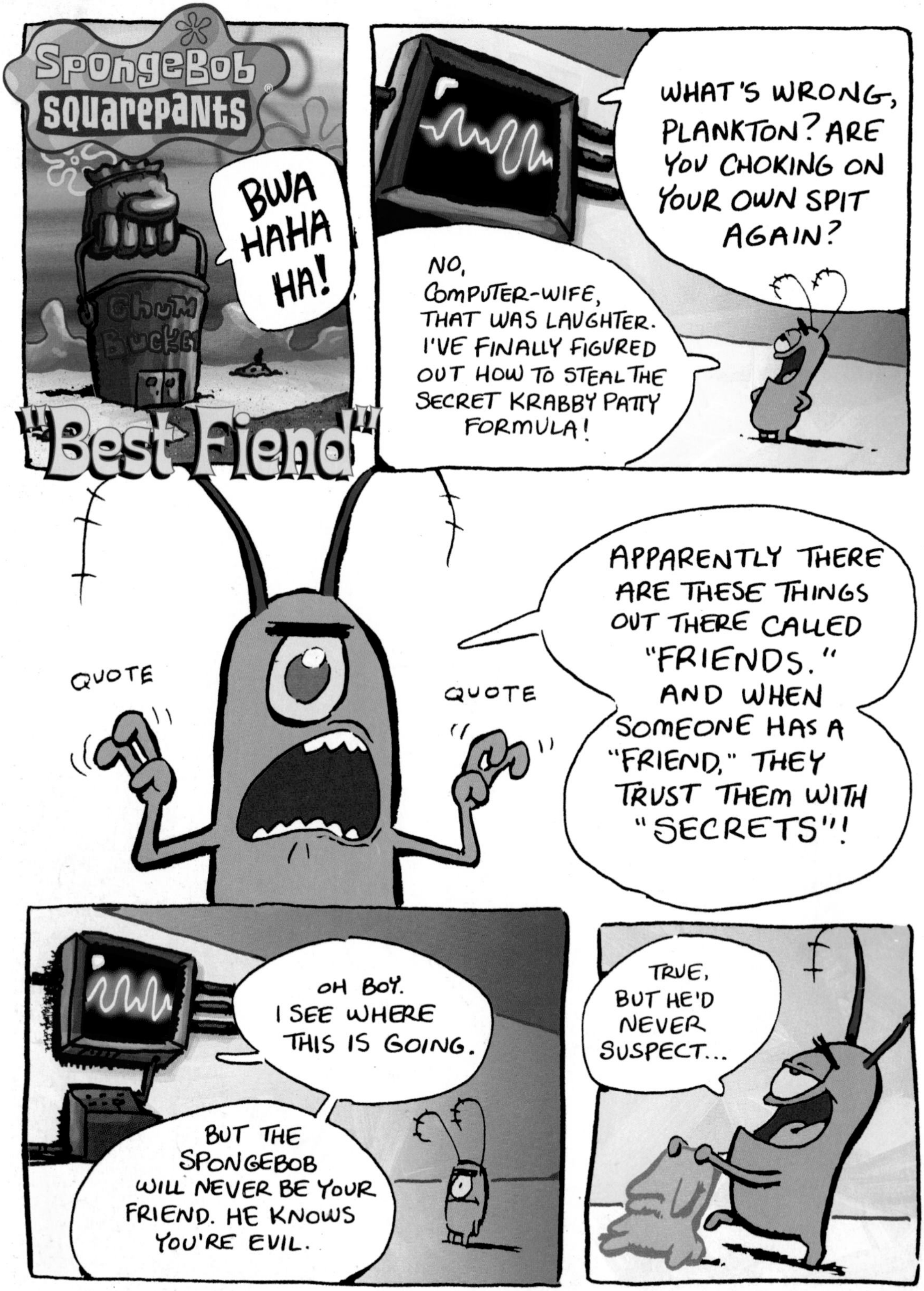
SpongeBob SquarePants
"Best Fiend"
Chum Bucket
BWA HAHA HA!
WHAT'S WRONG, PLANKTON? ARE YOU CHOKING ON YOUR OWN SPIT AGAIN?
NO, COMPUTER-WIFE, THAT WAS LAUGHTER. I'VE FINALLY FIGURED OUT HOW TO STEAL THE SECRET KRABBY PATTY FORMULA!
QUOTE
QUOTE
APPARENTLY THERE ARE THESE THINGS OUT THERE CALLED "FRIENDS." AND WHEN SOMEONE HAS A "FRIEND," THEY TRUST THEM WITH "SECRETS"!
OH BOY. I SEE WHERE THIS IS GOING.
BUT THE SPONGEBOB WILL NEVER BE YOUR FRIEND. HE KNOWS YOU'RE EVIL.
TRUE, BUT HE'D NEVER SUSPECT...

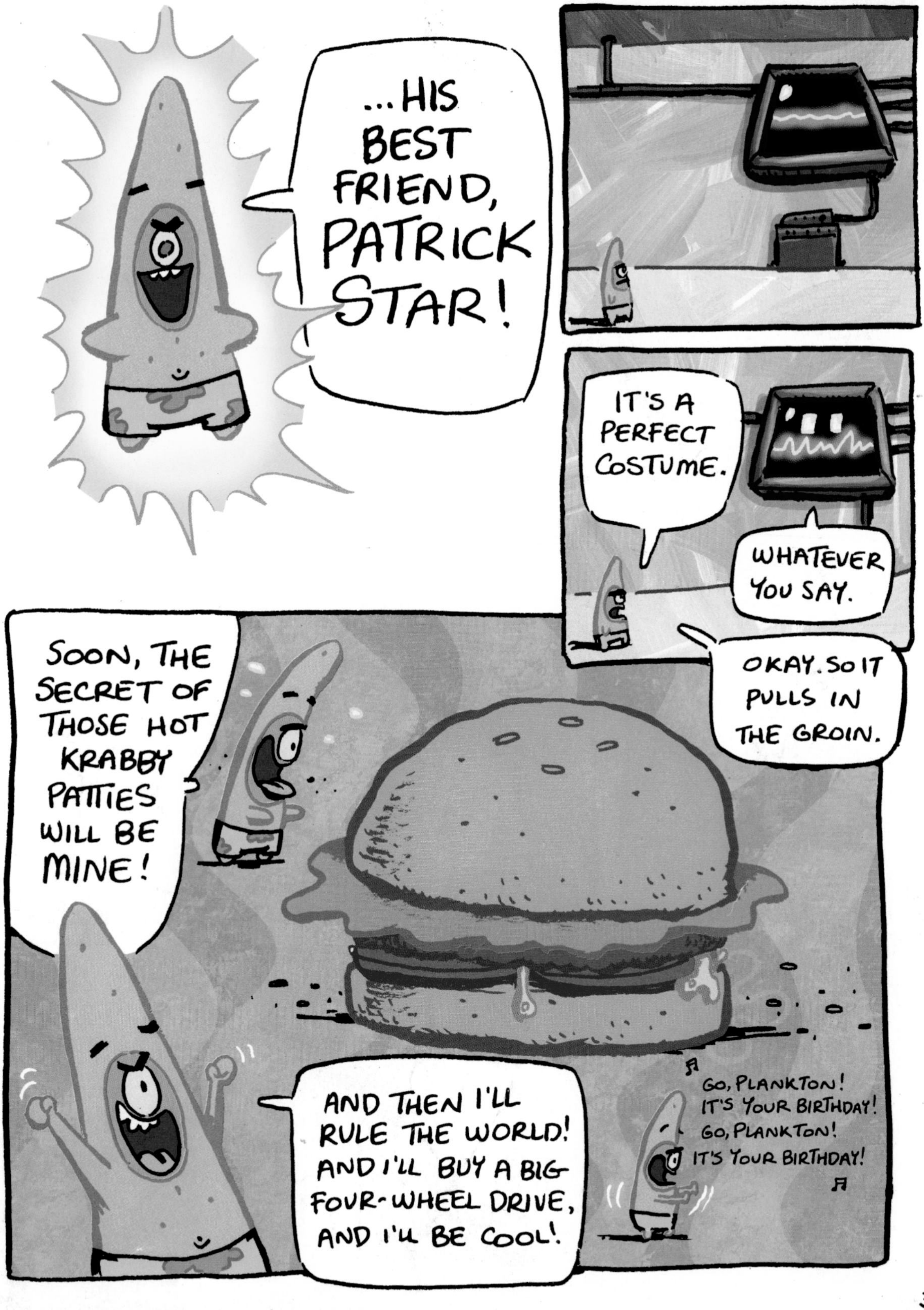
...HIS BEST FRIEND, PATRICK STAR!
IT'S A PERFECT COSTUME.
WHATEVER YOU SAY.
OKAY. SO IT PULLS IN THE GROIN.
SOON, THE SECRET OF THOSE HOT KRABBY PATTIES WILL BE MINE!
AND THEN I'LL RULE THE WORLD! AND I'LL BUY A BIG FOUR-WHEEL DRIVE, AND I'LL BE COOL!
GO, PLANKTON! IT'S YOUR BIRTHDAY! GO, PLANKTON! IT'S YOUR BIRTHDAY!

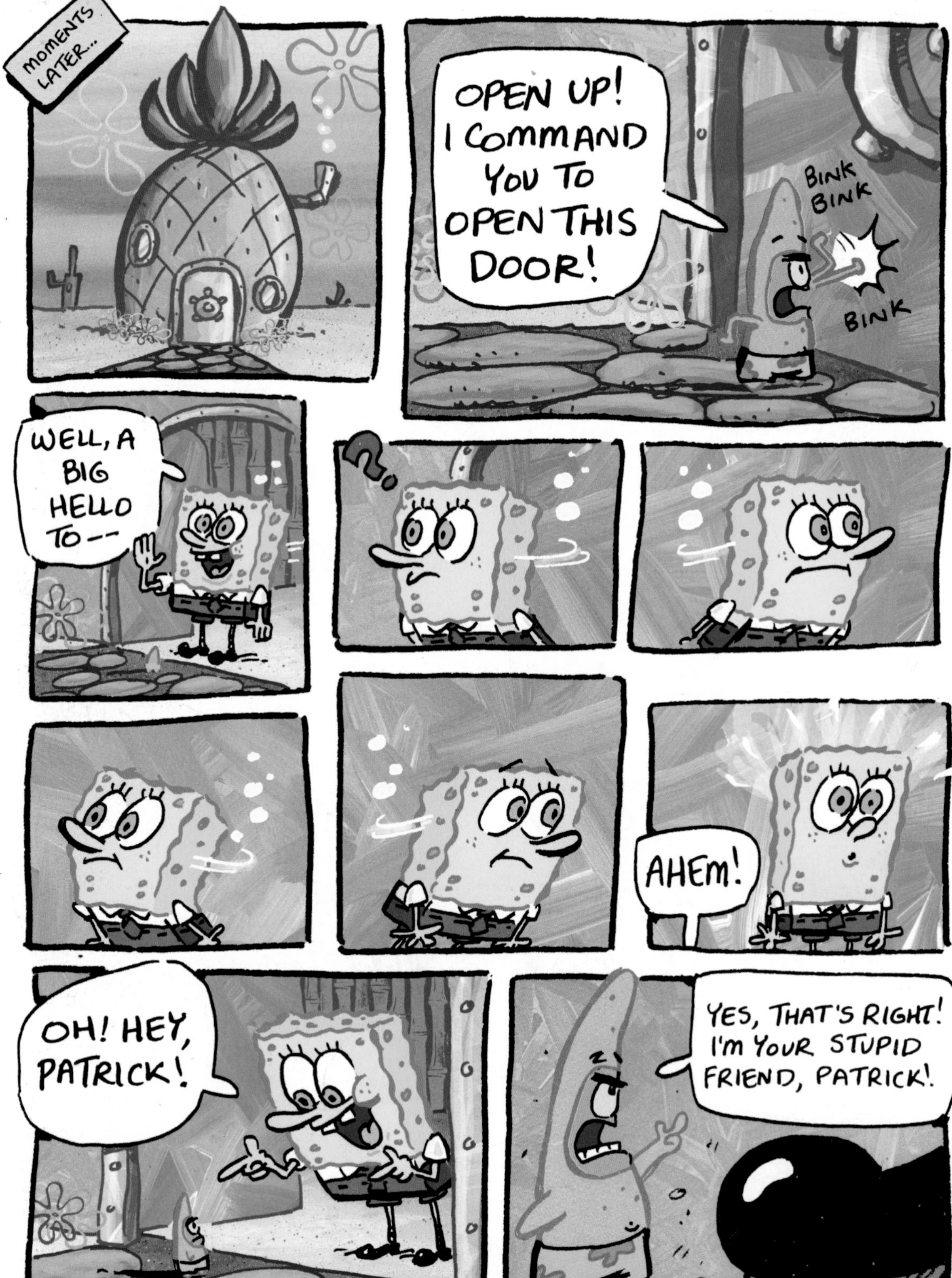
MOMENTS LATER...
OPEN UP! I COMMAND YOU TO OPEN THIS DOOR!
BINK BINK
BINK
WELL, A BIG HELLO TO--
AHEM!
OH! HEY, PATRICK!
YES, THAT'S RIGHT! I'M YOUR STUPID FRIEND, PATRICK!

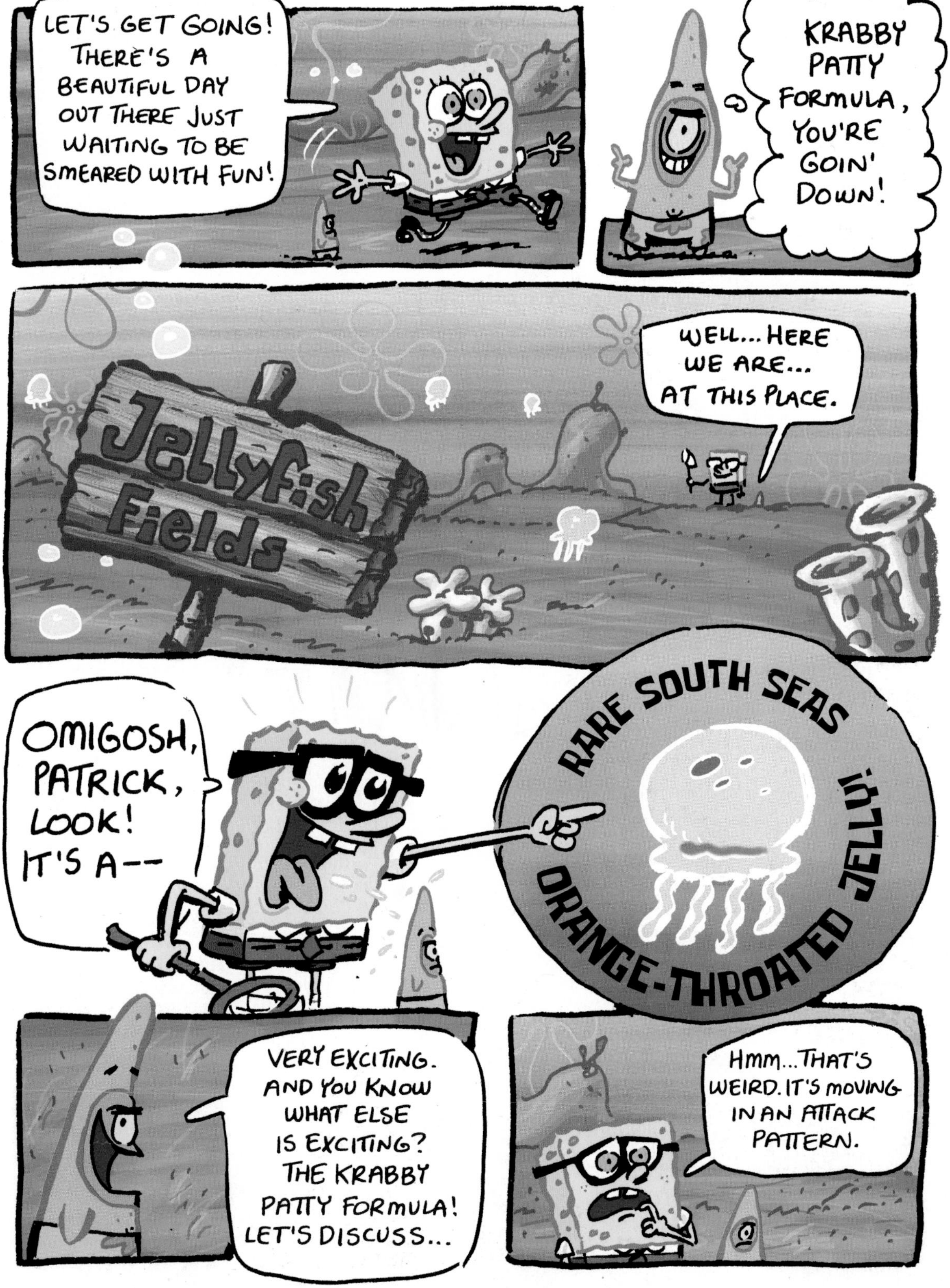
LET'S GET GOING! THERE'S A BEAUTIFUL DAY OUT THERE JUST WAITING TO BE SMEARED WITH FUN!
KRABBY PATTY FORMULA, YOU'RE GOIN' DOWN!
Jellyfish Fields
WELL... HERE WE ARE... AT THIS PLACE.
OMIGOSH, PATRICK, LOOK! IT'S A--
RARE SOUTH SEAS ORANGE-THROATED JELLY!
VERY EXCITING. AND YOU KNOW WHAT ELSE IS EXCITING? THE KRABBY PATTY FORMULA! LET'S DISCUSS...
HMM... THAT'S WEIRD. IT'S MOVING IN AN ATTACK PATTERN.

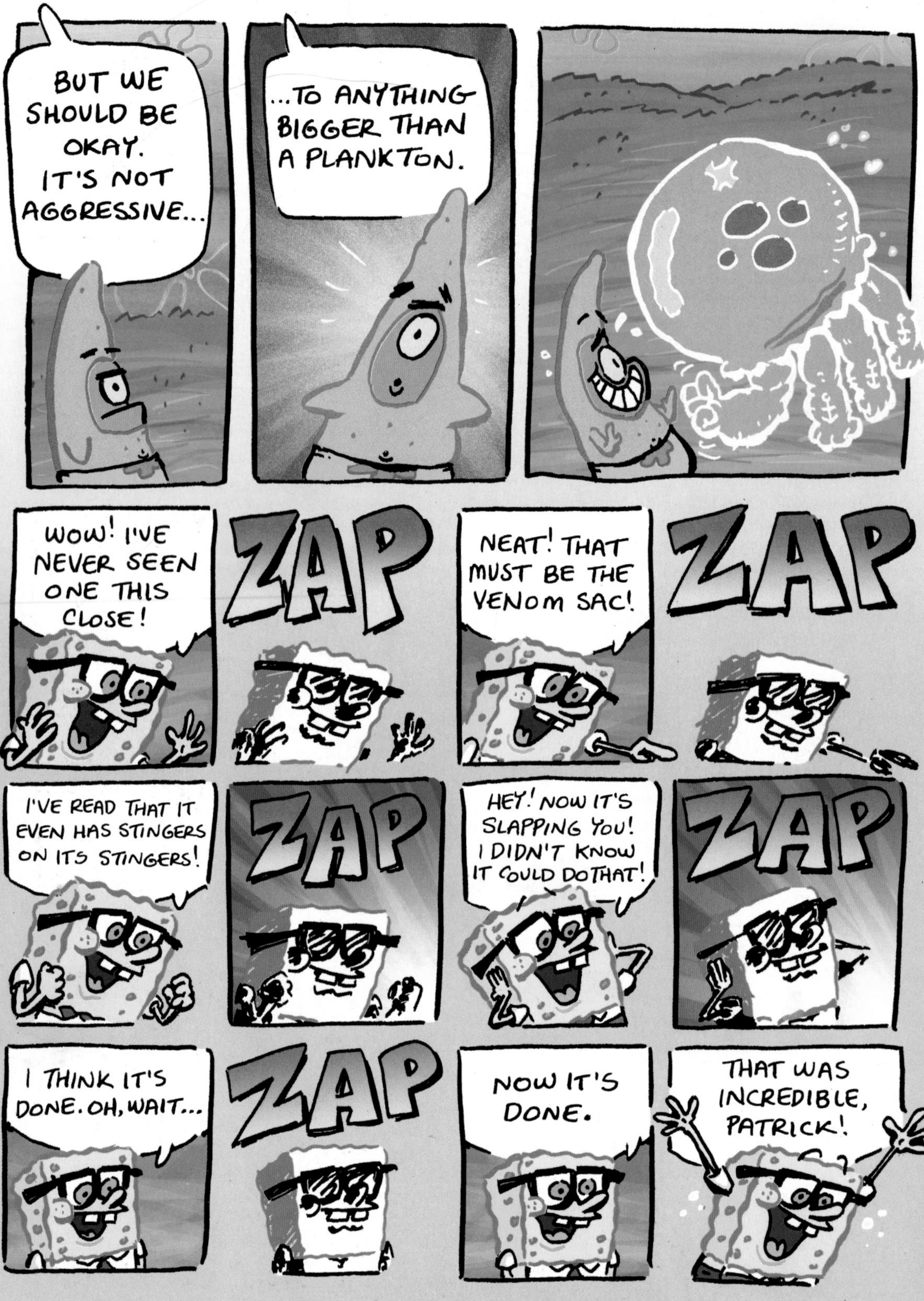
BUT WE SHOULD BE OKAY. IT'S NOT AGGRESSIVE...
...TO ANYTHING BIGGER THAN A PLANKTON.
WOW! I'VE NEVER SEEN ONE THIS CLOSE!
ZAP
NEAT! THAT MUST BE THE VENOM SAC!
ZAP
I'VE READ THAT IT EVEN HAS STINGERS ON ITS STINGERS!
ZAP
HEY! NOW IT'S SLAPPING YOU! I DIDN'T KNOW IT COULD DO THAT!
ZAP
I THINK IT'S DONE. OH, WAIT...
ZAP
NOW IT'S DONE.
THAT WAS INCREDIBLE, PATRICK!

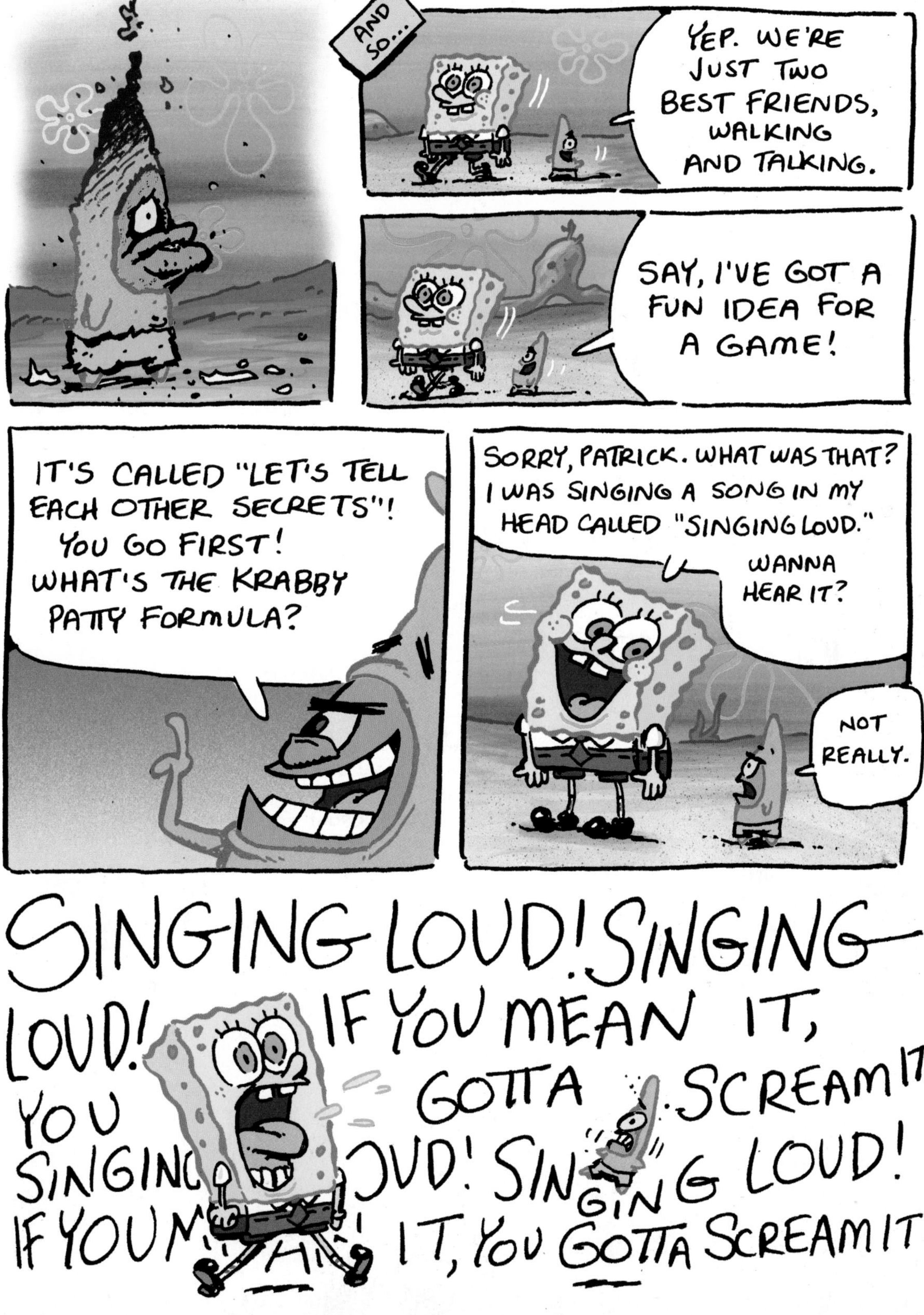
AND SO...
YEP. WE'RE JUST TWO BEST FRIENDS, WALKING AND TALKING.
SAY, I'VE GOT A FUN IDEA FOR A GAME!
IT'S CALLED "LET'S TELL EACH OTHER SECRETS"! YOU GO FIRST! WHAT'S THE KRABBY PATTY FORMULA?
SORRY, PATRICK. WHAT WAS THAT? I WAS SINGING A SONG IN MY HEAD CALLED "SINGING LOUD."
WANNA HEAR IT?
NOT REALLY.
SINGING LOUD! SINGING
LOUD! IF YOU MEAN IT,
YOU GOTTA SCREAM IT!
SINGIN OUD! SIN GIN G LOUD!
IF YOU M IT, YOU GOTTA SCREAM IT!

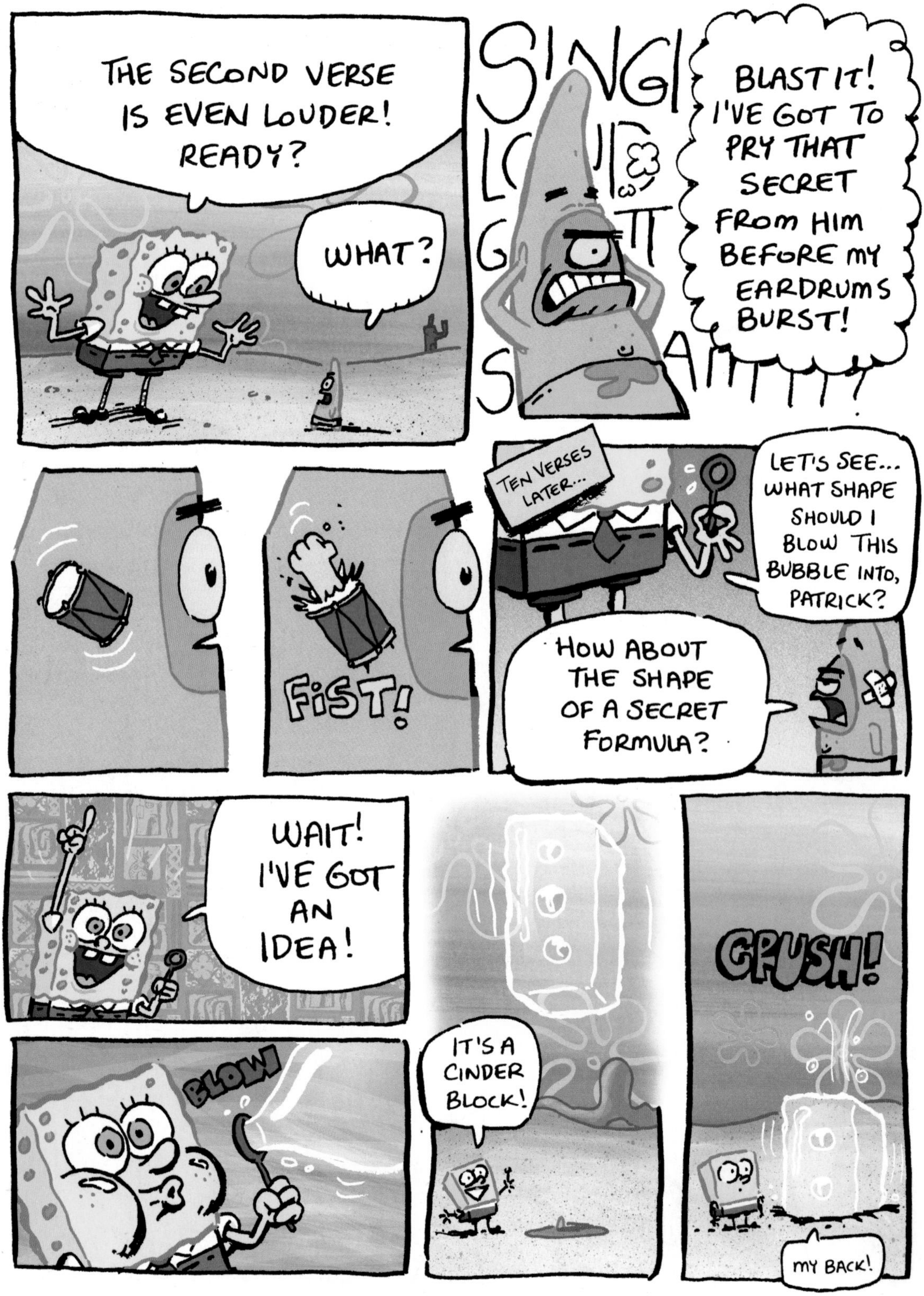
THE SECOND VERSE IS EVEN LOUDER! READY?
WHAT?
BLAST IT! I'VE GOT TO PRY THAT SECRET FROM HIM BEFORE MY EARDRUMS BURST!
FIST!
TEN VERSES LATER...
LET'S SEE... WHAT SHAPE SHOULD I BLOW THIS BUBBLE INTO, PATRICK?
HOW ABOUT THE SHAPE OF A SECRET FORMULA?
WAIT! I'VE GOT AN IDEA!
BLOW
IT'S A CINDER BLOCK!
CRUSH!
MY BACK!

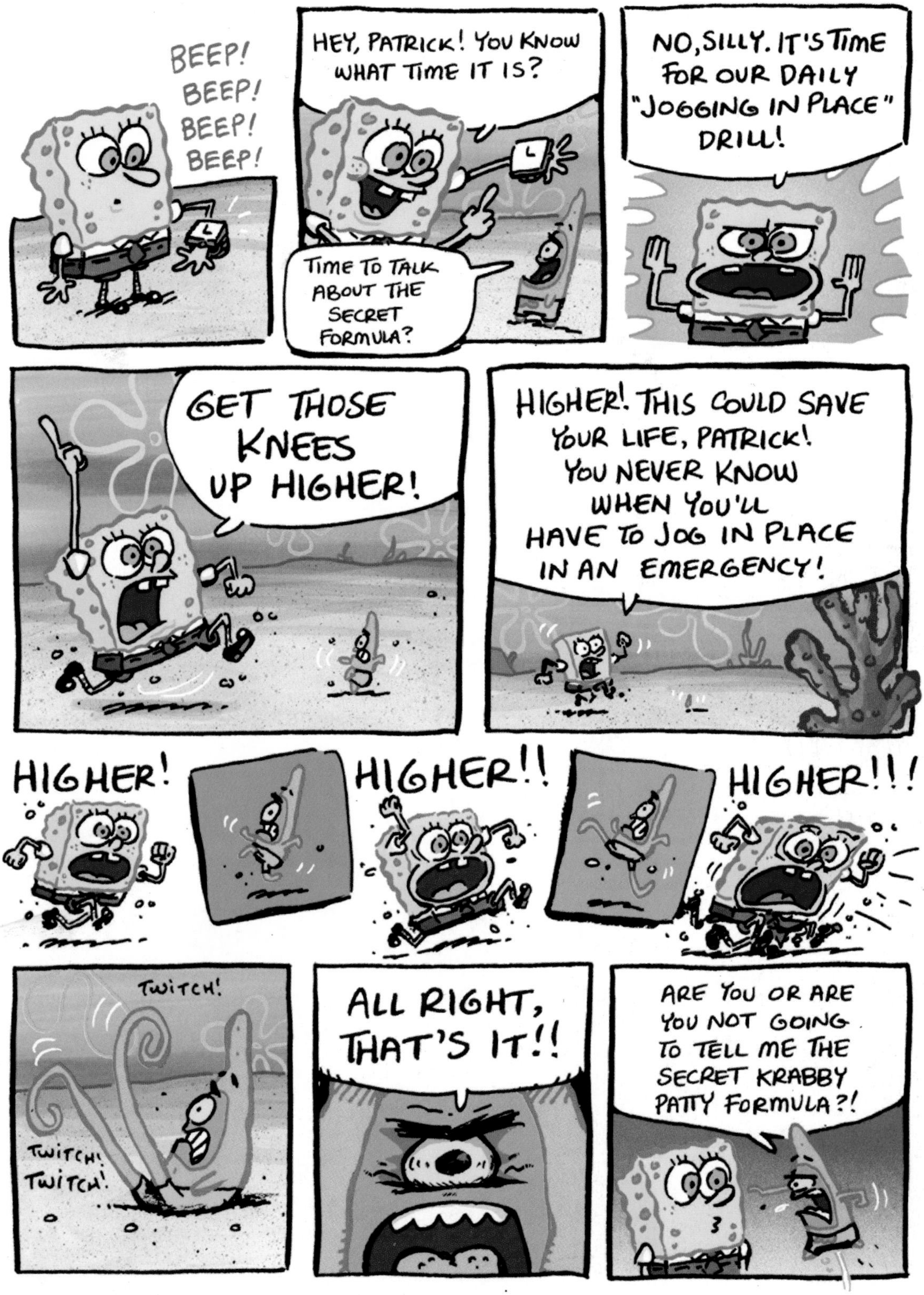
BEEP! BEEP! BEEP! BEEP!
HEY, PATRICK! YOU KNOW WHAT TIME IT IS?
TIME TO TALK ABOUT THE SECRET FORMULA?
NO, SILLY. IT'S TIME FOR OUR DAILY "JOGGING IN PLACE" DRILL!
GET THOSE KNEES UP HIGHER!
HIGHER! THIS COULD SAVE YOUR LIFE, PATRICK! YOU NEVER KNOW WHEN YOU'LL HAVE TO JOG IN PLACE IN AN EMERGENCY!
HIGHER!
HIGHER!!
HIGHER!!!
TWITCH!
TWITCH! TWITCH!
ALL RIGHT, THAT'S IT!!
ARE YOU OR ARE YOU NOT GOING TO TELL ME THE SECRET KRABBY PATTY FORMULA?!

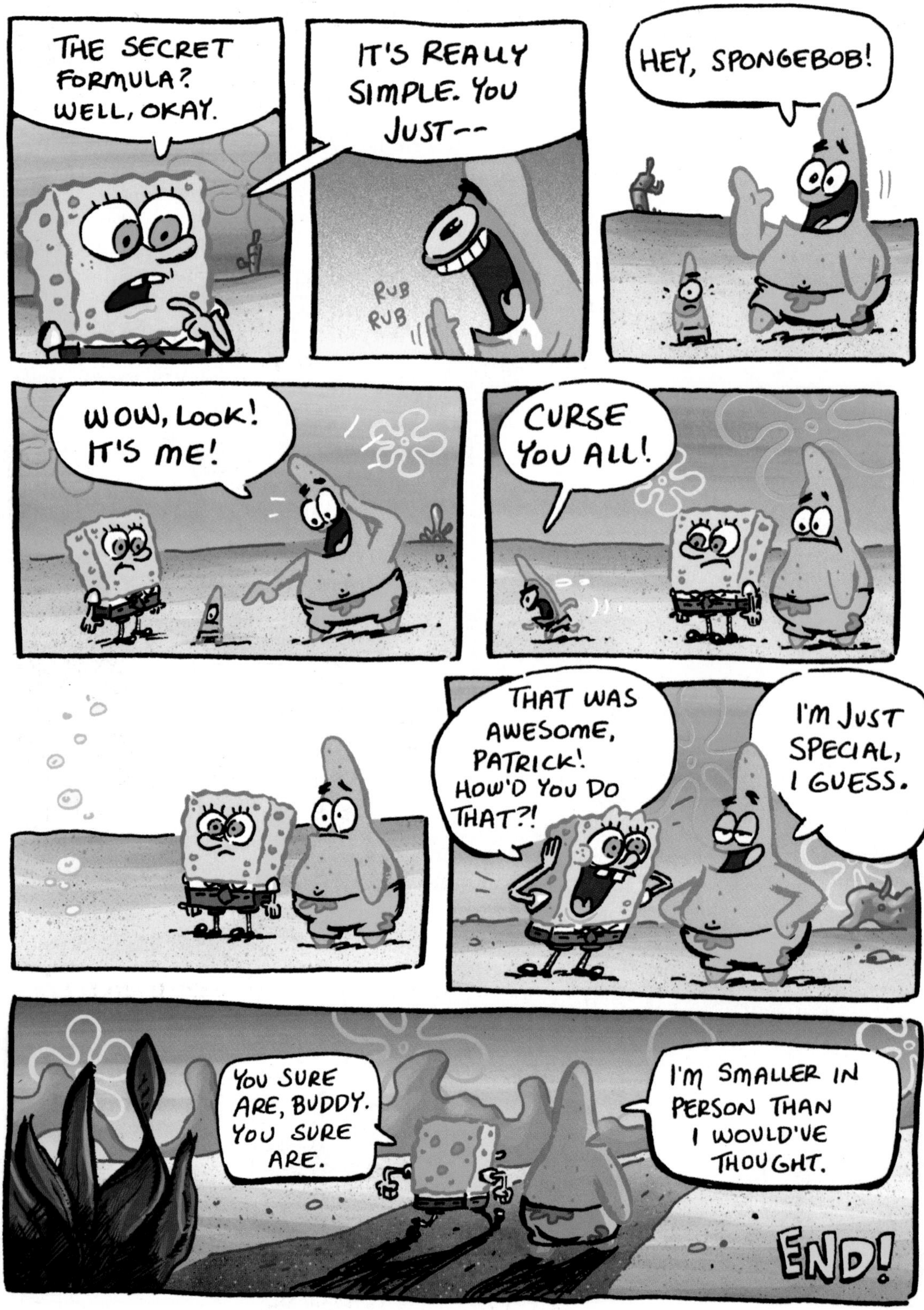
THE SECRET FORMULA? WELL, OKAY.
IT'S REALLY SIMPLE. YOU JUST--
RUB RUB
HEY, SPONGEBOB!
WOW, LOOK! IT'S ME!
CURSE YOU ALL!
THAT WAS AWESOME, PATRICK! HOW'D YOU DO THAT?!
I'M JUST SPECIAL, I GUESS.
YOU SURE ARE, BUDDY. YOU SURE ARE.
I'M SMALLER IN PERSON THAN I WOULD'VE THOUGHT.
END!

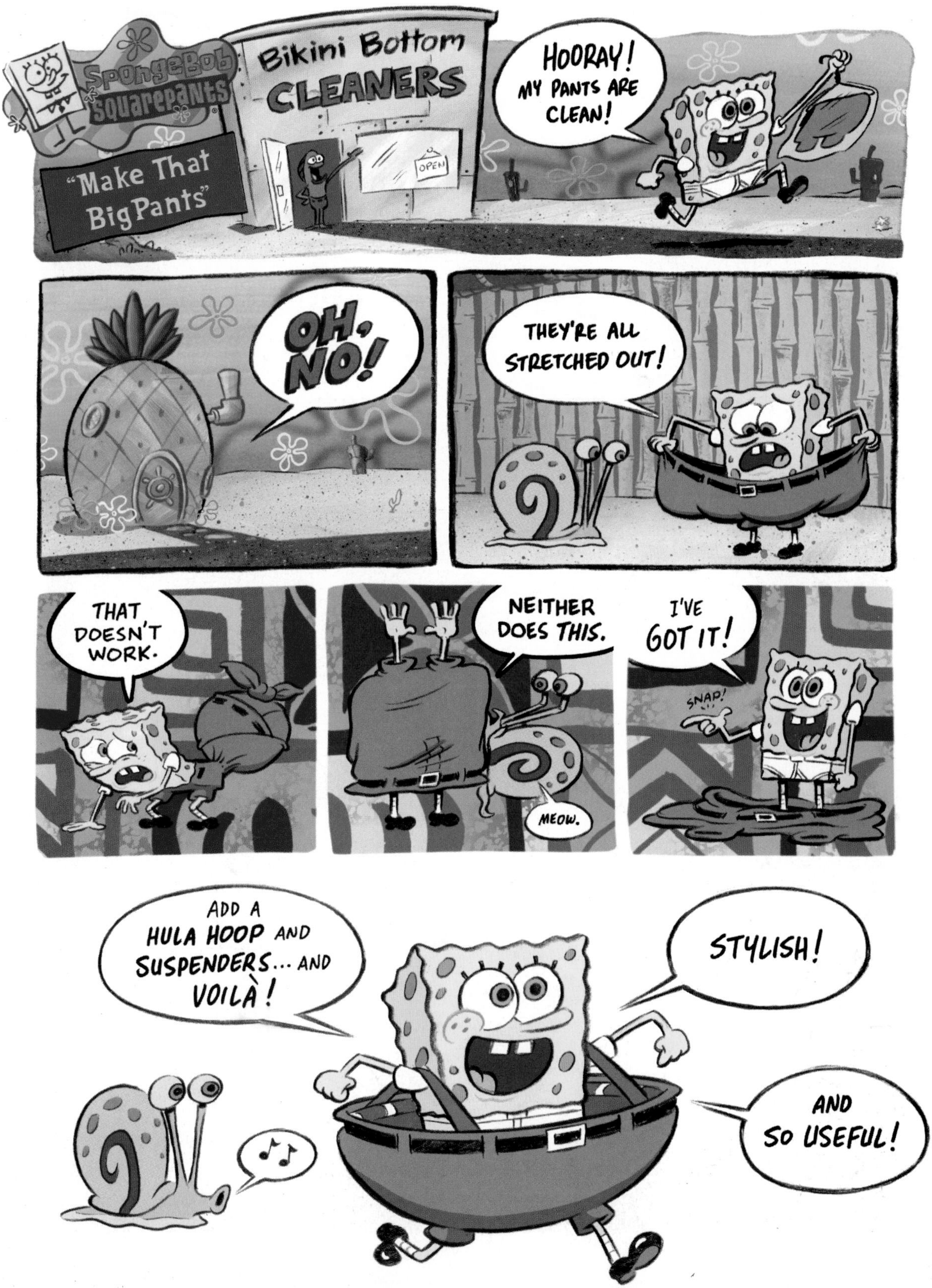

SpongeBob SquarePants
"Make That BigPants"
Bikini Bottom CLEANERS
OPEN
HOORAY! MY PANTS ARE CLEAN!
OH, NO!
THEY'RE ALL STRETCHED OUT!
THAT DOESN'T WORK.
NEITHER DOES THIS.
MEOW.
I'VE GOT IT!
SNAP!
ADD A HULA HOOP AND SUSPENDERS... AND VOILÀ!
STYLISH!
AND SO USEFUL!

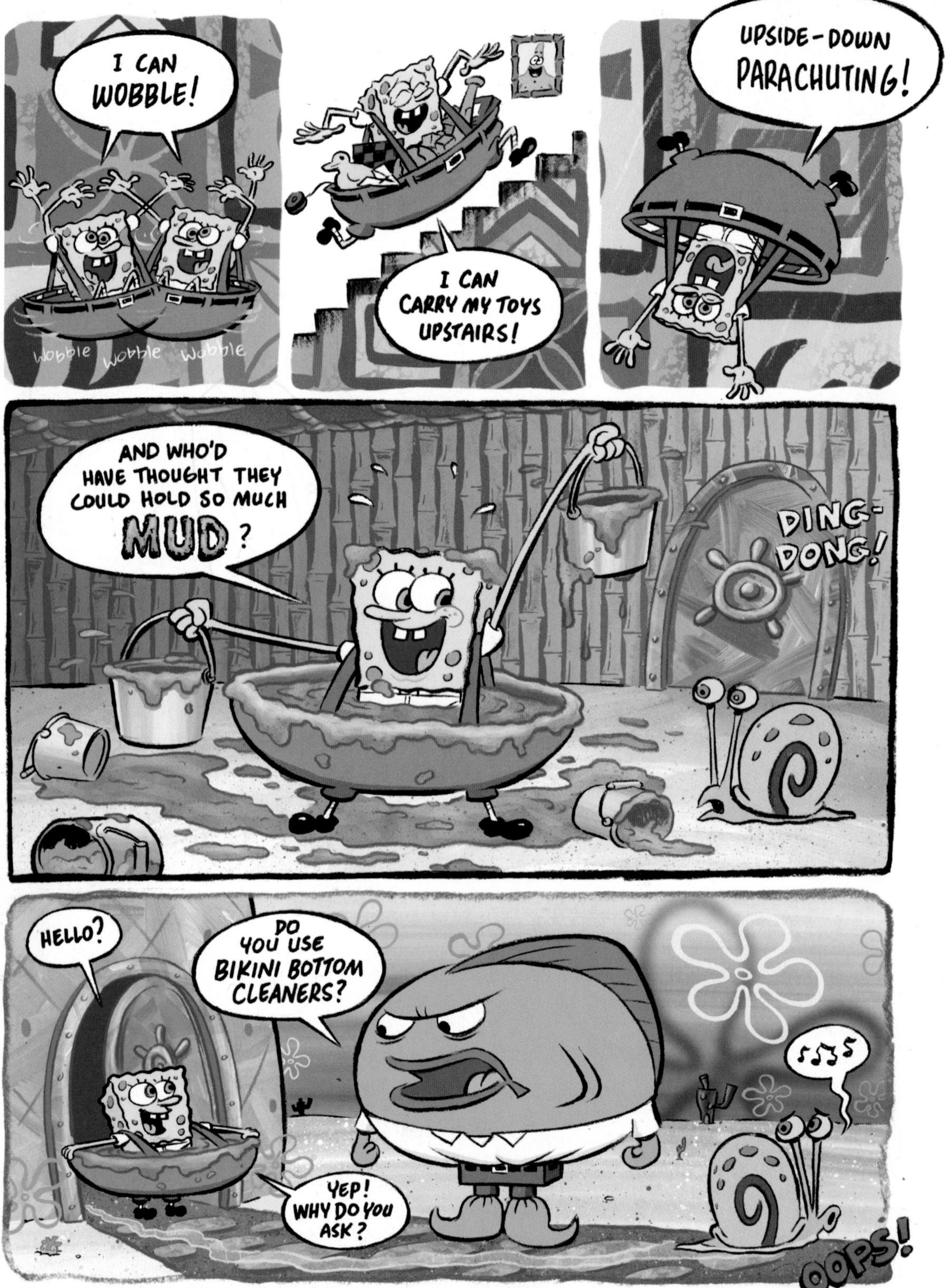

I CAN WOBBLE!
WOBBLE WOBBLE WOBBLE
I CAN CARRY MY TOYS UPSTAIRS!
UPSIDE-DOWN PARACHUTING!
AND WHO'D HAVE THOUGHT THEY COULD HOLD SO MUCH MUD?
DING-DONG!
HELLO?
DO YOU USE BIKINI BOTTOM CLEANERS?
YEP! WHY DO YOU ASK?
OOPS!

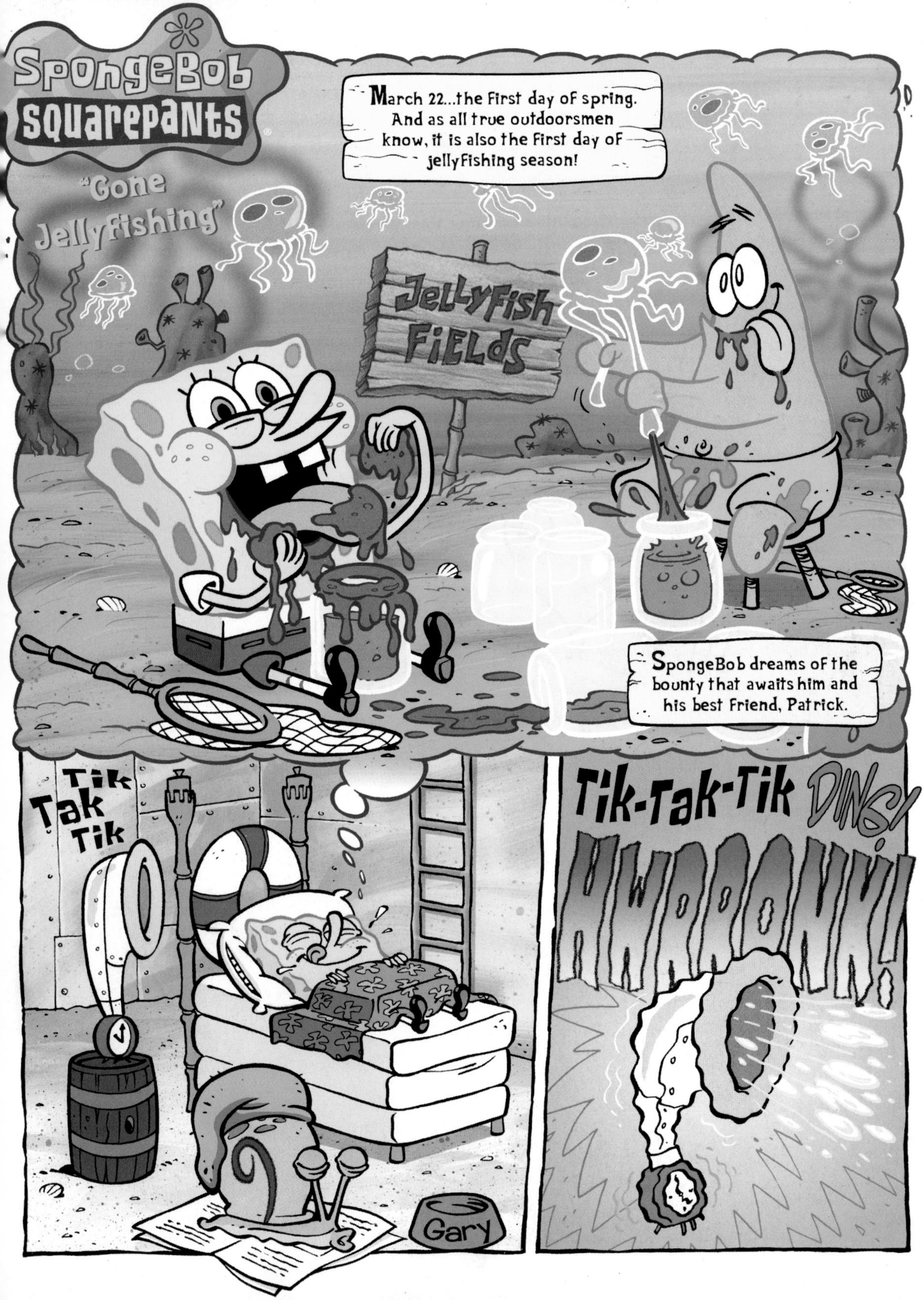
SpongeBob SquarePants®
"Gone JellyFishing"
March 22...the First day of spring. And as all true outdoorsmen know, it is also the First day of jellyFishing season!
JellyFish Fields
SpongeBob dreams of the bounty that awaits him and his best Friend, Patrick.
Tik Tak Tik
Gary
Tik-Tak-Tik DING!
HWAAONK!

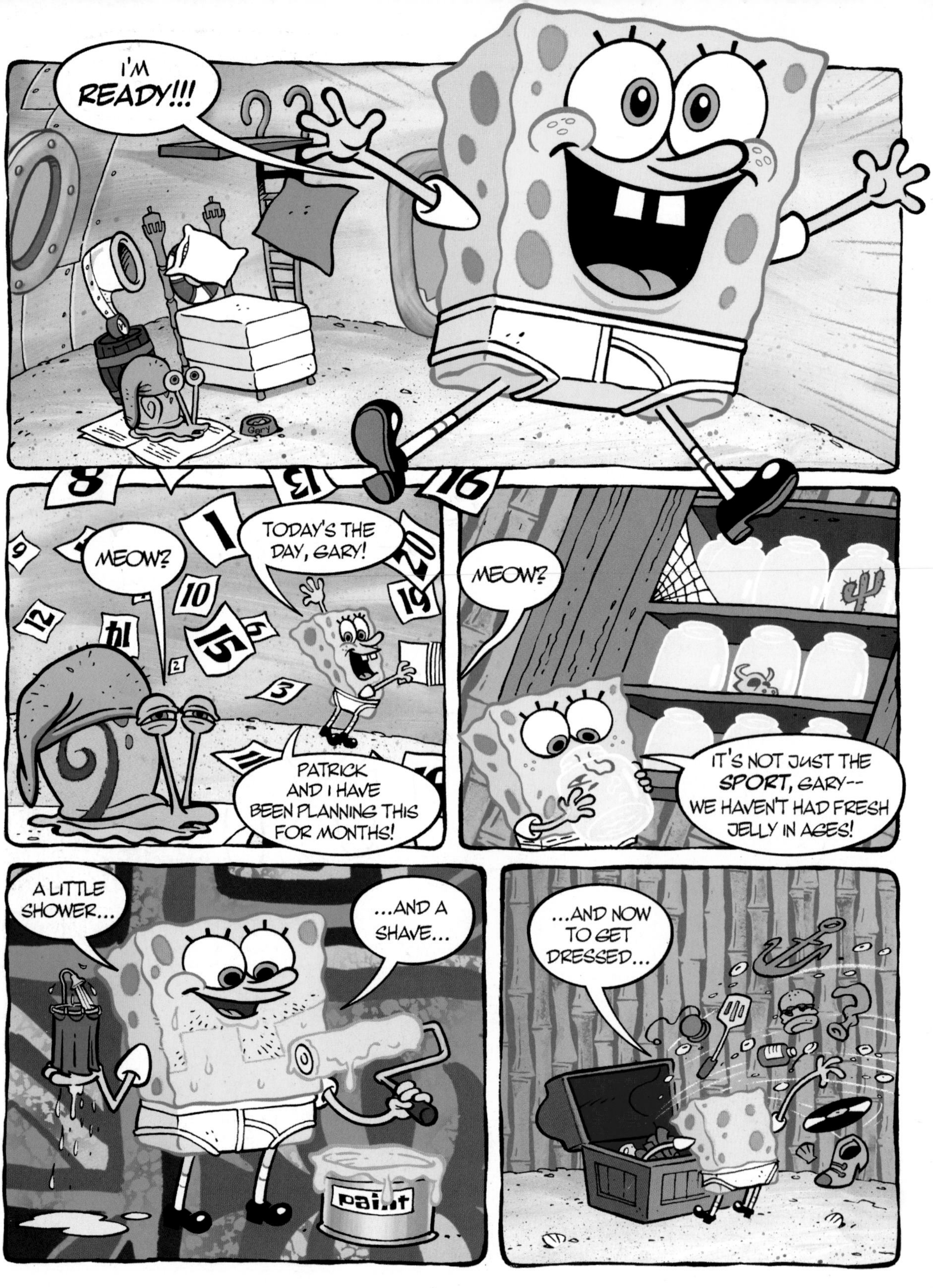
I'M READY!!!
MEOW?
TODAY'S THE DAY, GARY!
PATRICK AND I HAVE BEEN PLANNING THIS FOR MONTHS!
MEOW?
IT'S NOT JUST THE SPORT, GARY-- WE HAVEN'T HAD FRESH JELLY IN AGES!
A LITTLE SHOWER...
...AND A SHAVE...
...AND NOW TO GET DRESSED...

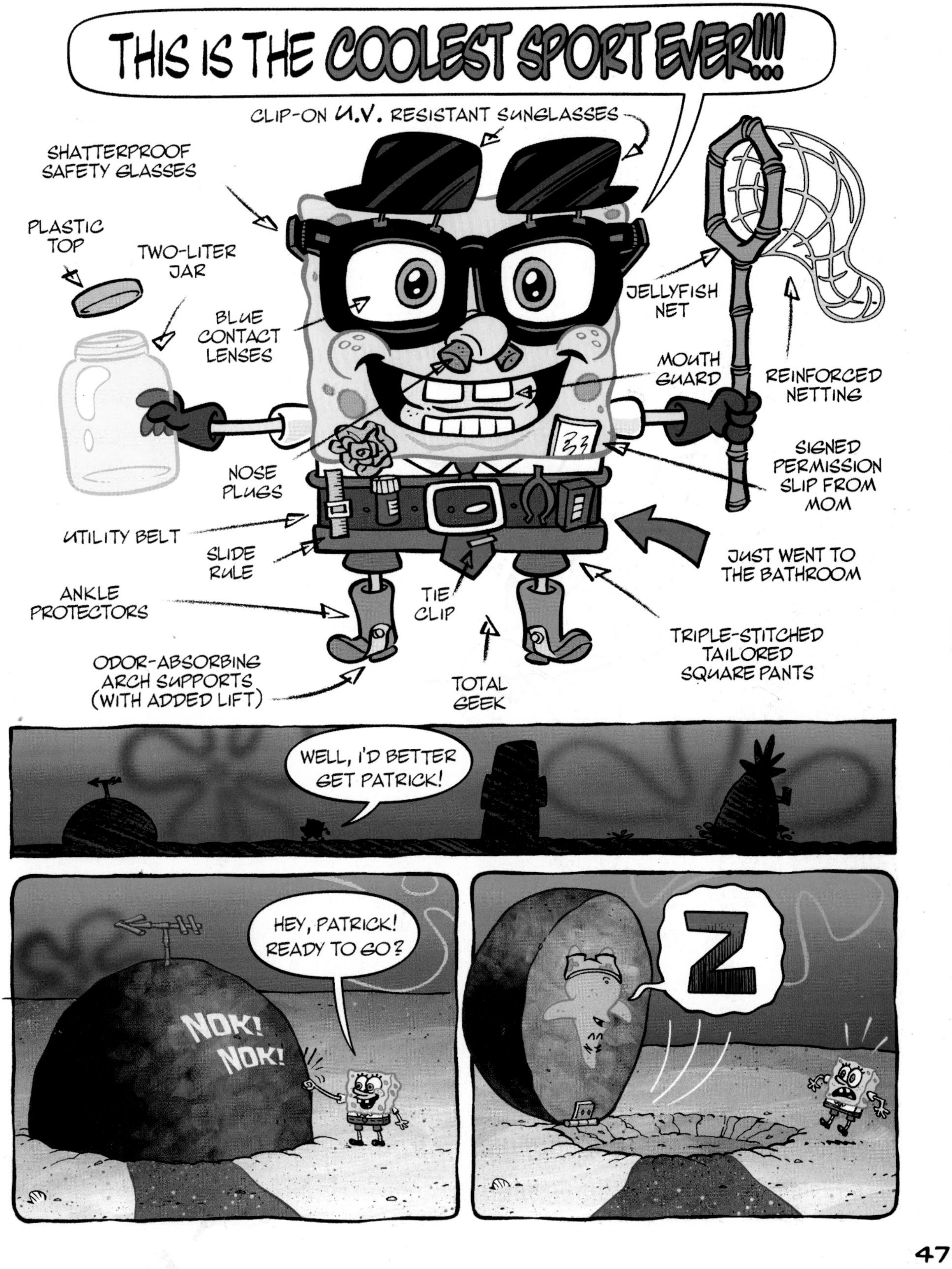
THIS IS THE COOLEST SPORT EVER!!!
CLIP-ON U.V. RESISTANT SUNGLASSES
SHATTERPROOF SAFETY GLASSES
PLASTIC TOP
TWO-LITER JAR
BLUE CONTACT LENSES
JELLYFISH NET
MOUTH GUARD
REINFORCED NETTING
SIGNED PERMISSION SLIP FROM MOM
NOSE PLUGS
UTILITY BELT
SLIDE RULE
JUST WENT TO THE BATHROOM
ANKLE PROTECTORS
TIE CLIP
TRIPLE-STITCHED TAILORED SQUARE PANTS
ODOR-ABSORBING ARCH SUPPORTS (WITH ADDED LIFT)
TOTAL GEEK
WELL, I'D BETTER GET PATRICK!
HEY, PATRICK! READY TO GO?
NOK! NOK!
Z

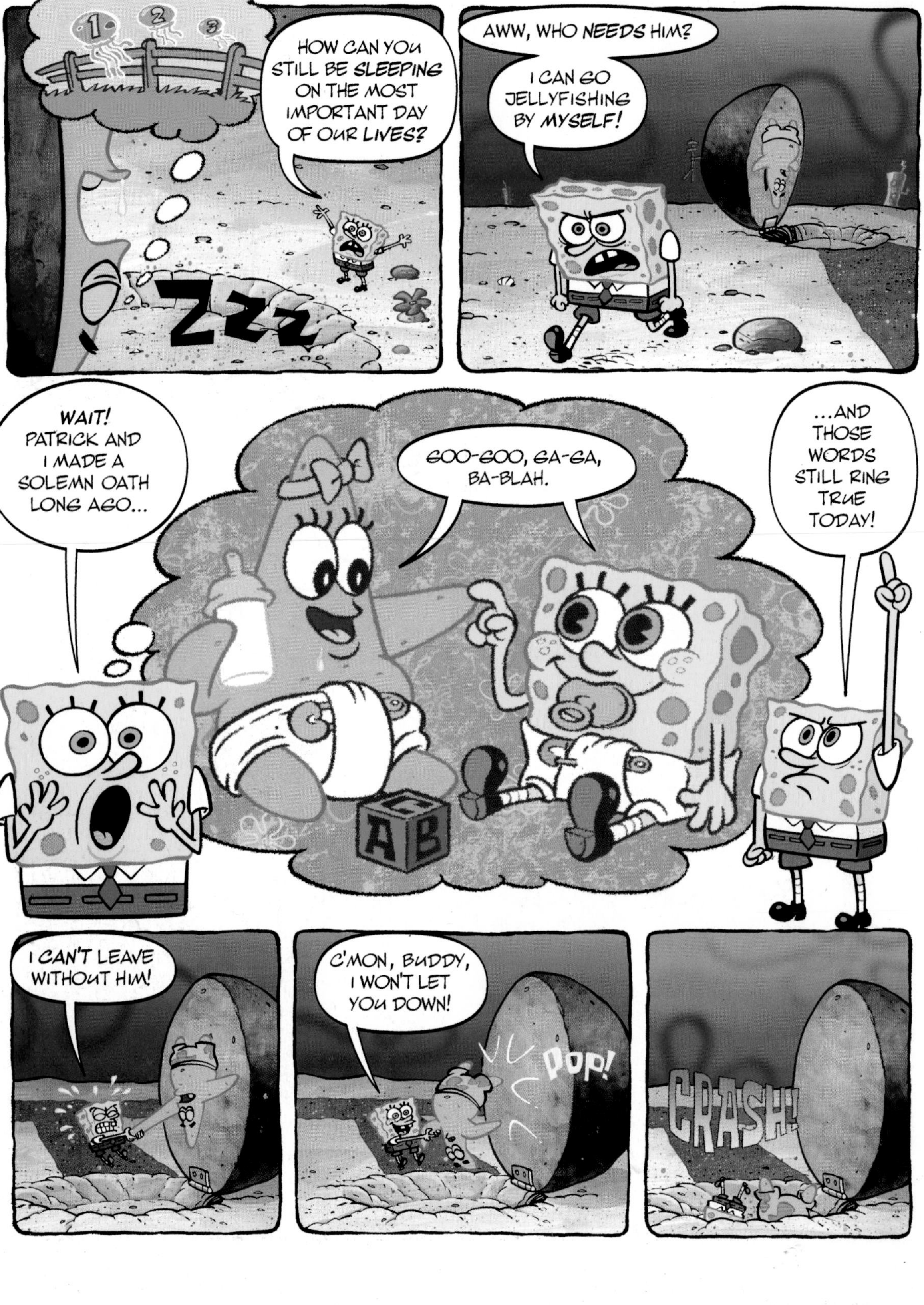
HOW CAN YOU STILL BE SLEEPING ON THE MOST IMPORTANT DAY OF OUR LIVES?
ZZZ
AWW, WHO NEEDS HIM?
I CAN GO JELLYFISHING BY MYSELF!
WAIT! PATRICK AND I MADE A SOLEMN OATH LONG AGO...
GOO-GOO, GA-GA, BA-BLAH.
...AND THOSE WORDS STILL RING TRUE TODAY!
I CAN'T LEAVE WITHOUT HIM!
C'MON, BUDDY, I WON'T LET YOU DOWN!
POP!
CRASH!

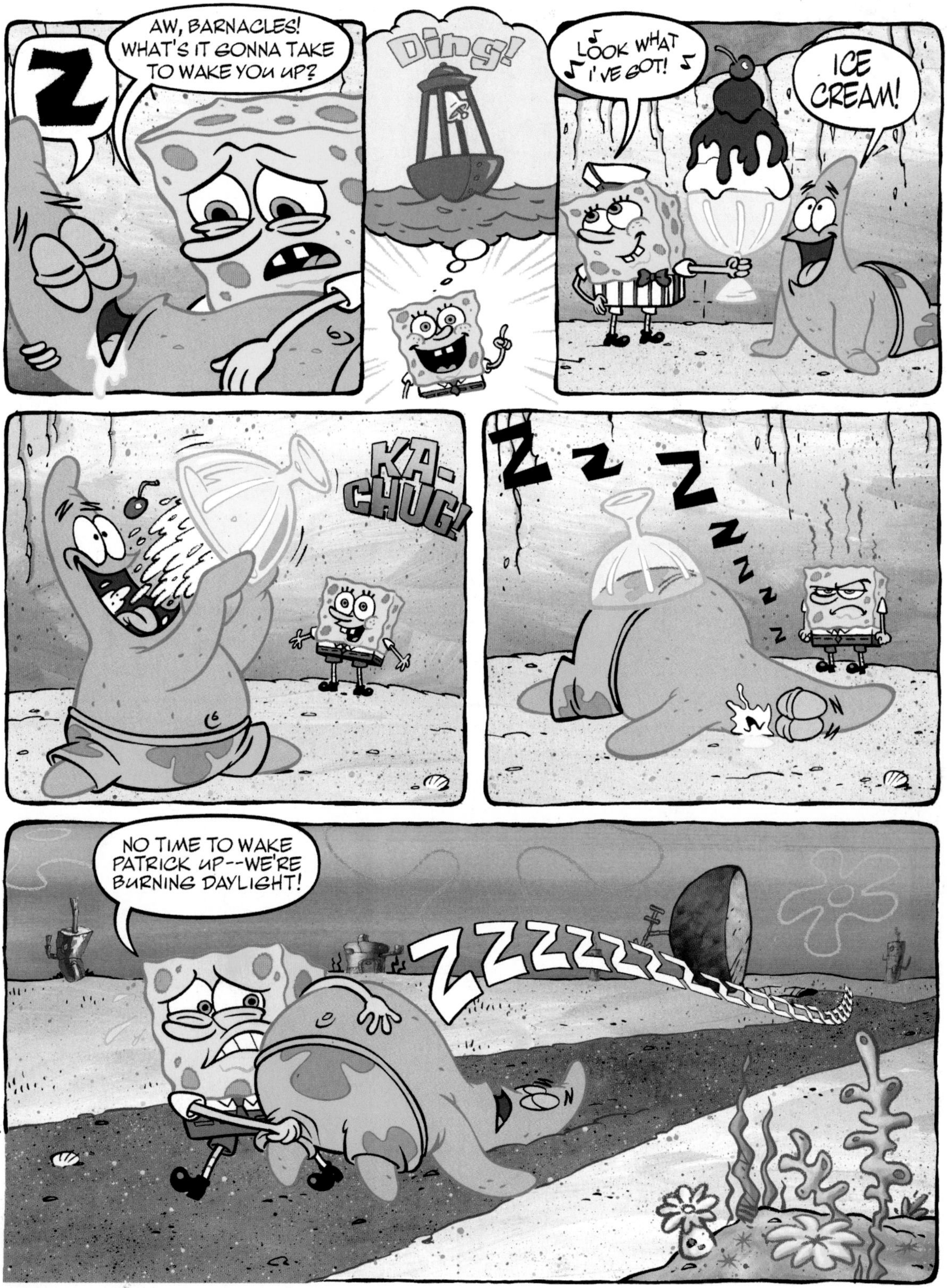
Z
AW, BARNACLES! WHAT'S IT GONNA TAKE TO WAKE YOU UP?
Ding!
LOOK WHAT I'VE GOT!
ICE CREAM!
KA-CHUG!
Z Z Z Z Z Z Z Z
NO TIME TO WAKE PATRICK UP--WE'RE BURNING DAYLIGHT!
ZZZZZZZZZZZZ

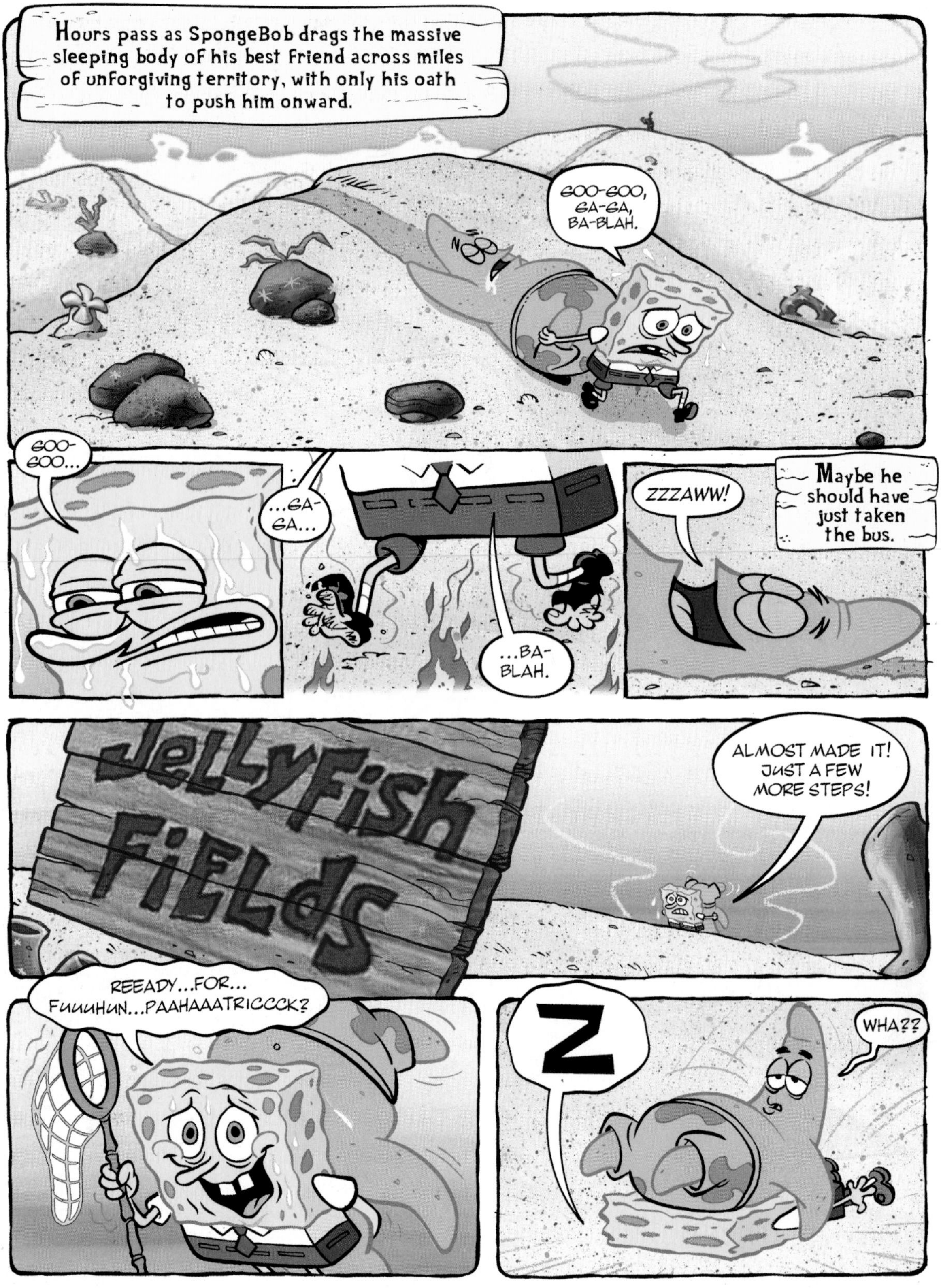

Hours pass as SpongeBob drags the massive sleeping body of his best friend across miles of unforgiving territory, with only his oath to push him onward.
GOO-GOO, GA-GA, BA-BLAH.
GOO-GOO...
...GA-GA...
...BA-BLAH.
ZZZAWW!
Maybe he should have just taken the bus.
JELLYFISH FIELDS
ALMOST MADE IT! JUST A FEW MORE STEPS!
REEADY...FOR... FUUUHUN...PAAHAAATRICCCK?
Z
WHA??

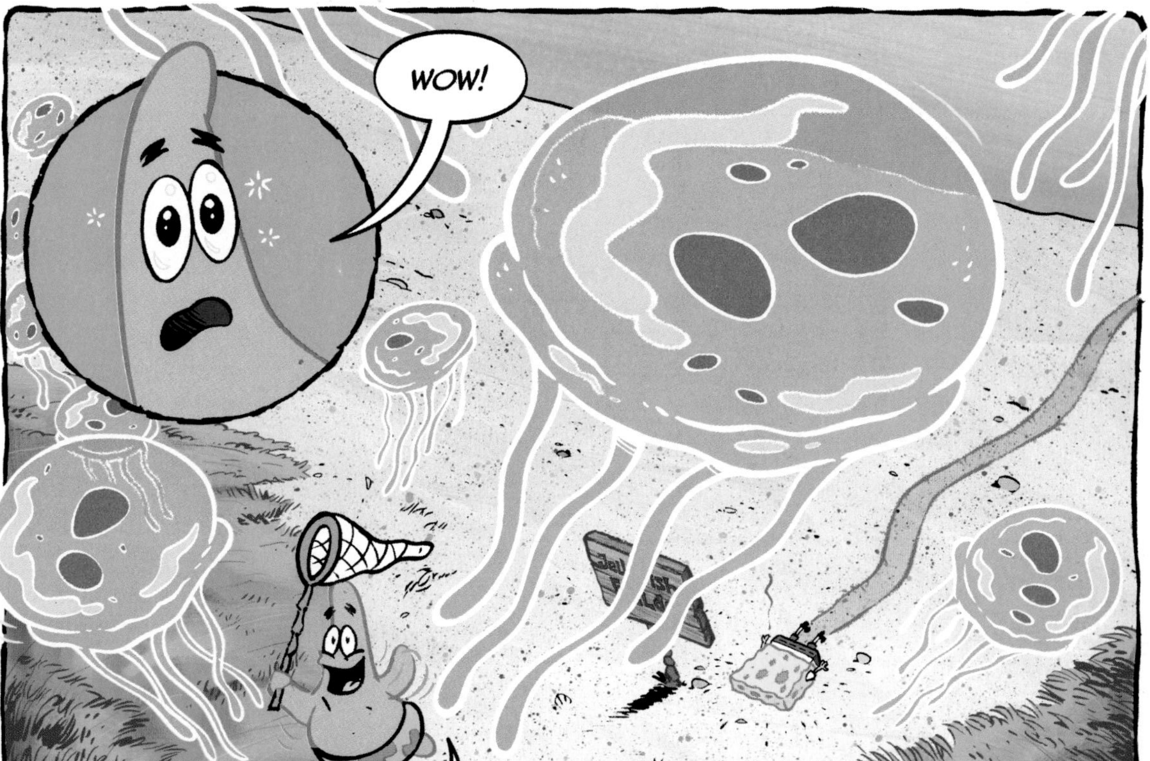
WOW!
MY DREAMS HAVE COME TRUE! WHOO-HOO!

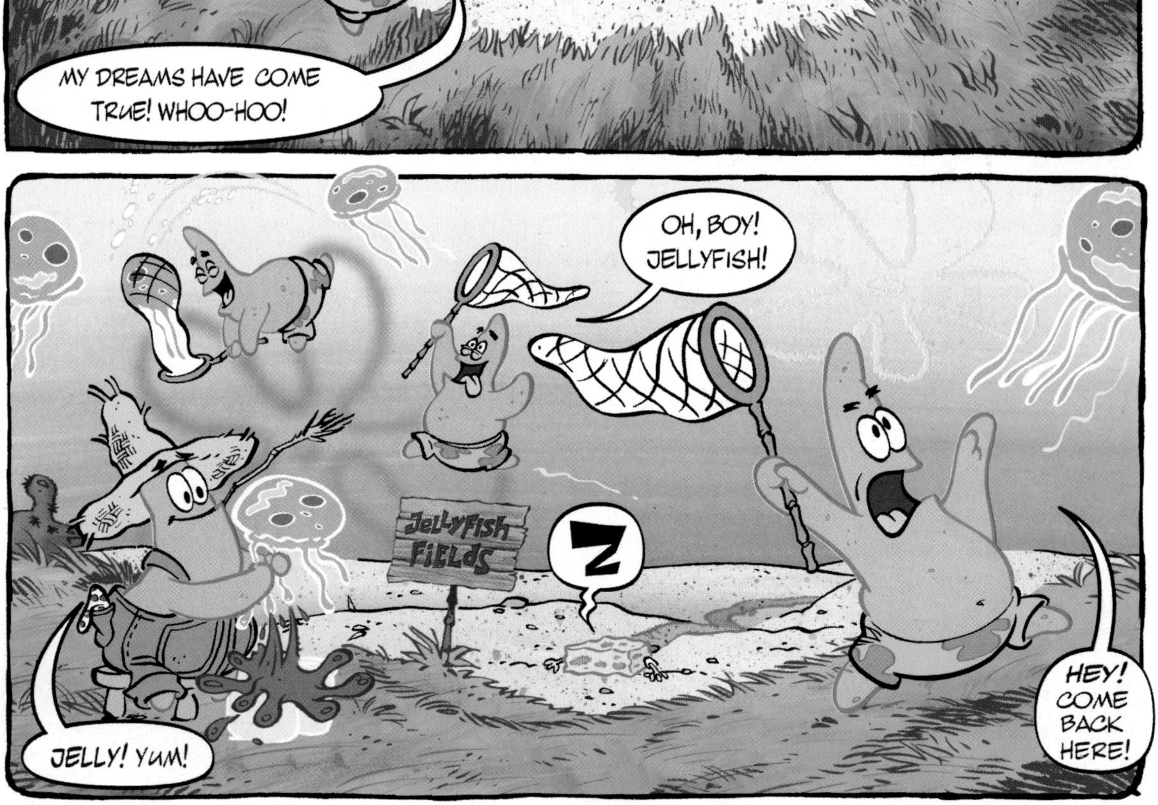
OH, BOY! JELLYFISH!
JELLYFISH FIELDS
Z
JELLY! YUM!
HEY! COME BACK HERE!

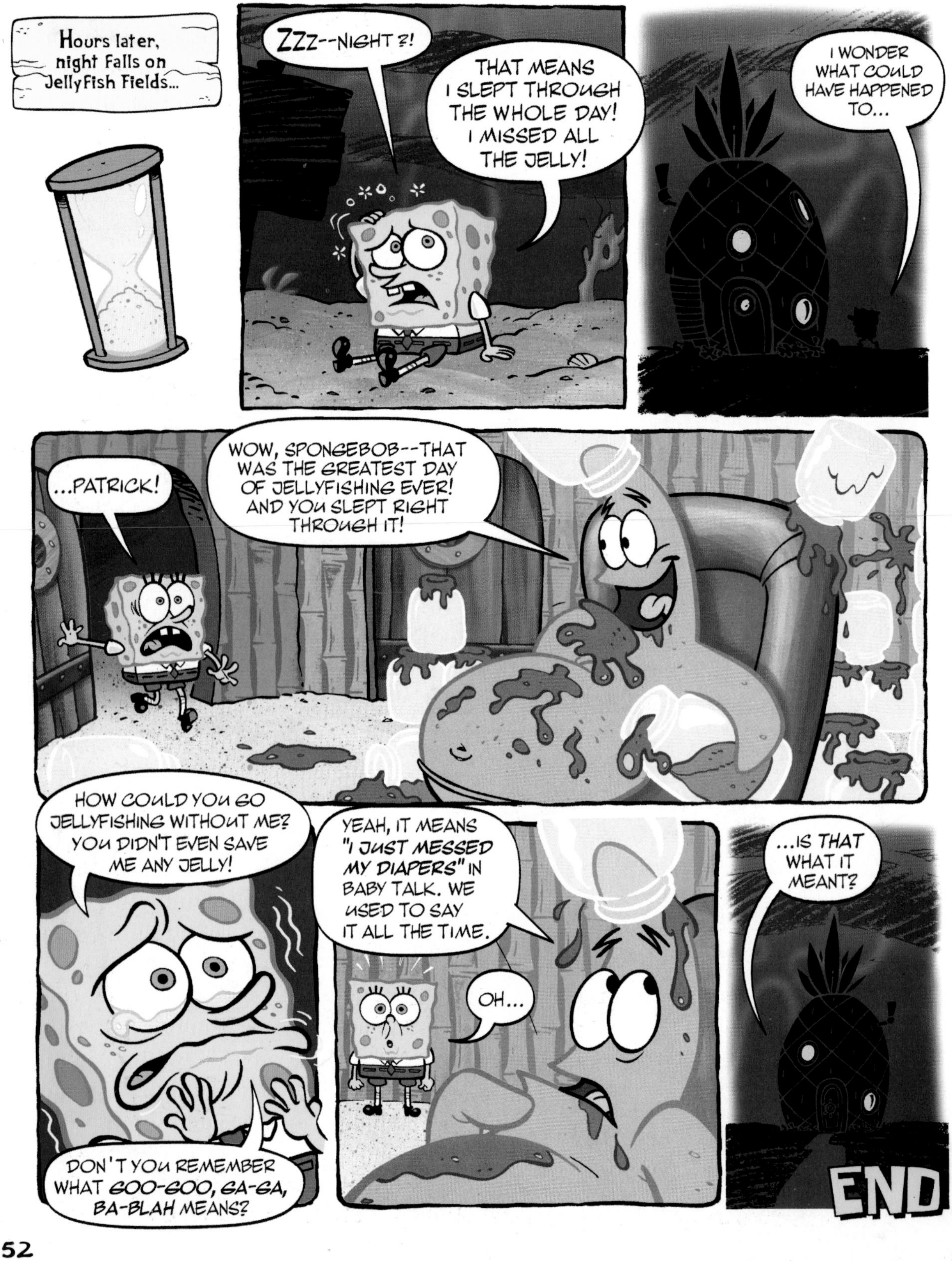
Hours later, night falls on Jellyfish Fields...
ZZZ--NIGHT?!
THAT MEANS I SLEPT THROUGH THE WHOLE DAY! I MISSED ALL THE JELLY!
I WONDER WHAT COULD HAVE HAPPENED TO...
...PATRICK!
WOW, SPONGEBOB--THAT WAS THE GREATEST DAY OF JELLYFISHING EVER! AND YOU SLEPT RIGHT THROUGH IT!
HOW COULD YOU GO JELLYFISHING WITHOUT ME? YOU DIDN'T EVEN SAVE ME ANY JELLY!
DON'T YOU REMEMBER WHAT GOO-GOO, GA-GA, BA-BLAH MEANS?
YEAH, IT MEANS "I JUST MESSED MY DIAPERS" IN BABY TALK. WE USED TO SAY IT ALL THE TIME.
OH...
...IS THAT WHAT IT MEANT?
END

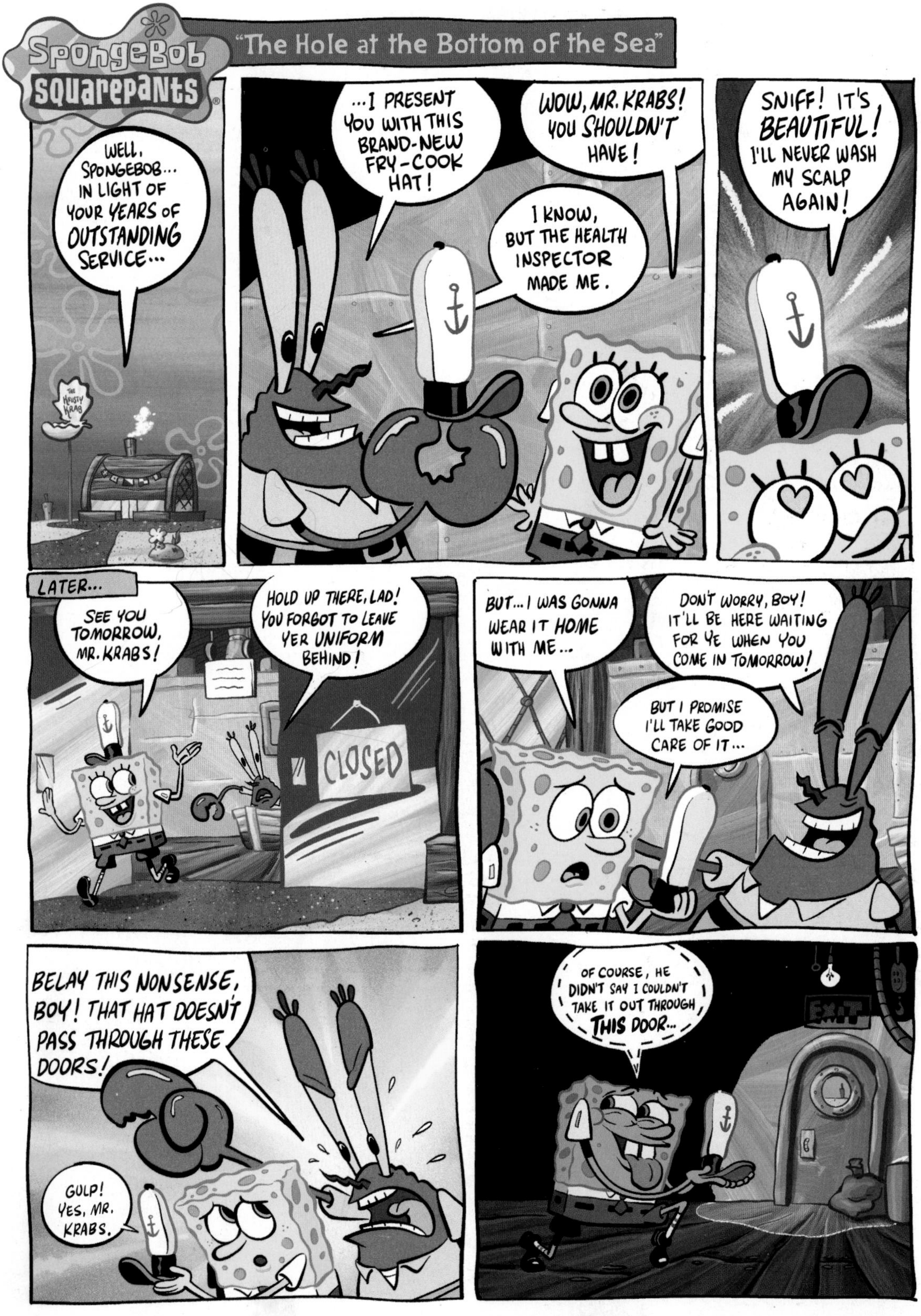
SpongeBob SquarePants
"The Hole at the Bottom of the Sea"
WELL, SPONGEBOB... IN LIGHT OF YOUR YEARS OF OUTSTANDING SERVICE...
...I PRESENT YOU WITH THIS BRAND-NEW FRY-COOK HAT!
WOW, MR. KRABS! YOU SHOULDN'T HAVE!
I KNOW, BUT THE HEALTH INSPECTOR MADE ME.
SNIFF! IT'S BEAUTIFUL! I'LL NEVER WASH MY SCALP AGAIN!
LATER...
SEE YOU TOMORROW, MR. KRABS!
HOLD UP THERE, LAD! YOU FORGOT TO LEAVE YER UNIFORM BEHIND!
CLOSED
BUT... I WAS GONNA WEAR IT HOME WITH ME...
DON'T WORRY, BOY! IT'LL BE HERE WAITING FOR YE WHEN YOU COME IN TOMORROW!
BUT I PROMISE I'LL TAKE GOOD CARE OF IT...
BELAY THIS NONSENSE, BOY! THAT HAT DOESN'T PASS THROUGH THESE DOORS!
GULP! YES, MR. KRABS.
OF COURSE, HE DIDN'T SAY I COULDN'T TAKE IT OUT THROUGH THIS DOOR...
EXIT

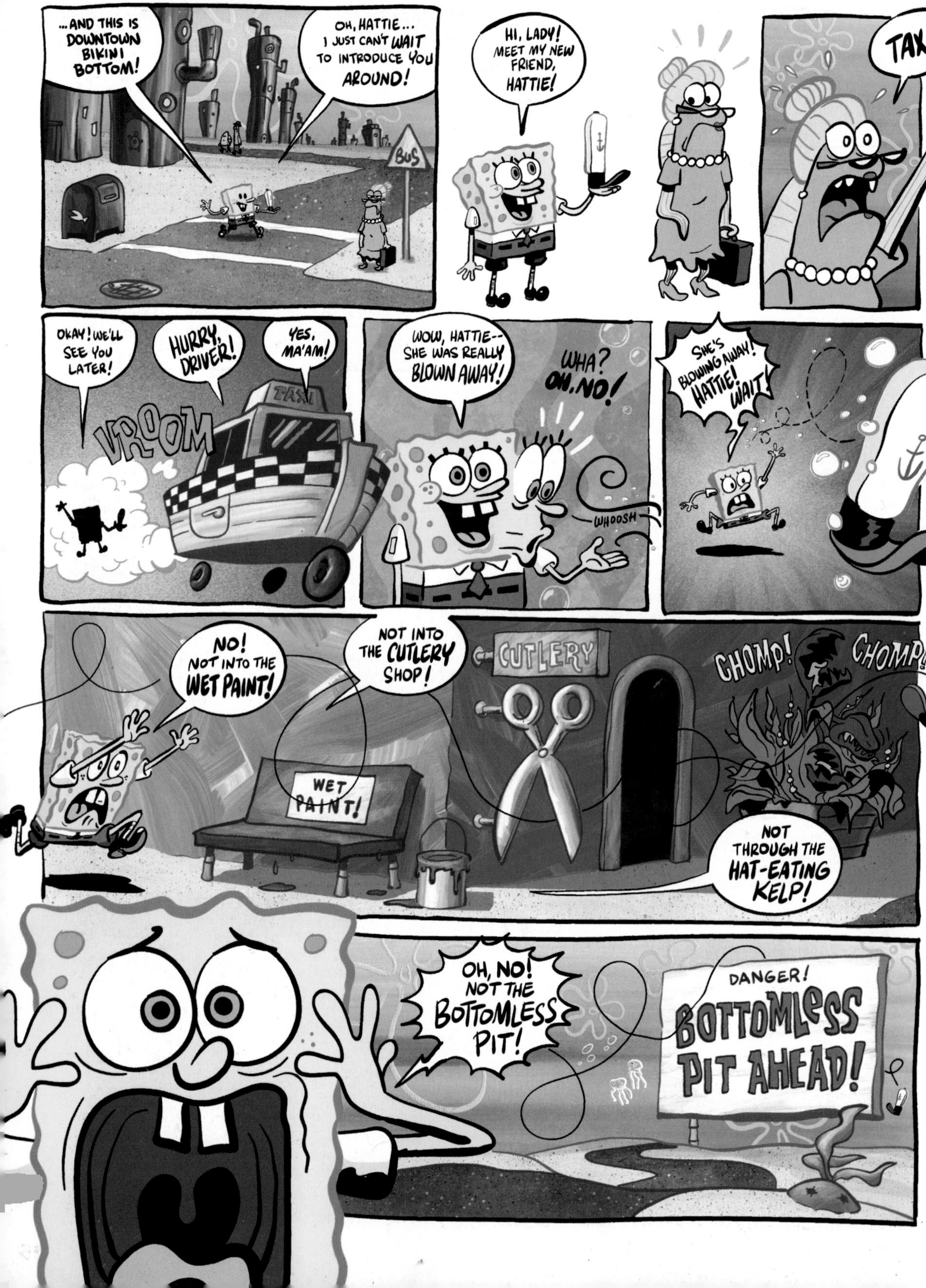
...AND THIS IS DOWNTOWN BIKINI BOTTOM!
OH, HATTIE... I JUST CAN'T WAIT TO INTRODUCE YOU AROUND!
BUS
HI, LADY! MEET MY NEW FRIEND, HATTIE!
TAXI!
OKAY! WE'LL SEE YOU LATER!
HURRY, DRIVER!
YES, MA'AM!
VROOM
TAXI
WOW, HATTIE-- SHE WAS REALLY BLOWN AWAY!
WHA? OH, NO!
WHOOSH
SHE'S BLOWING AWAY! HATTIE! WAIT!
NO! NOT INTO THE WET PAINT!
WET PAINT!
NOT INTO THE CUTLERY SHOP!
CUTLERY
CHOMP! CHOMP!
NOT THROUGH THE HAT-EATING KELP!
OH, NO! NOT THE BOTTOMLESS PIT!
DANGER!
BOTTOMLESS PIT AHEAD!

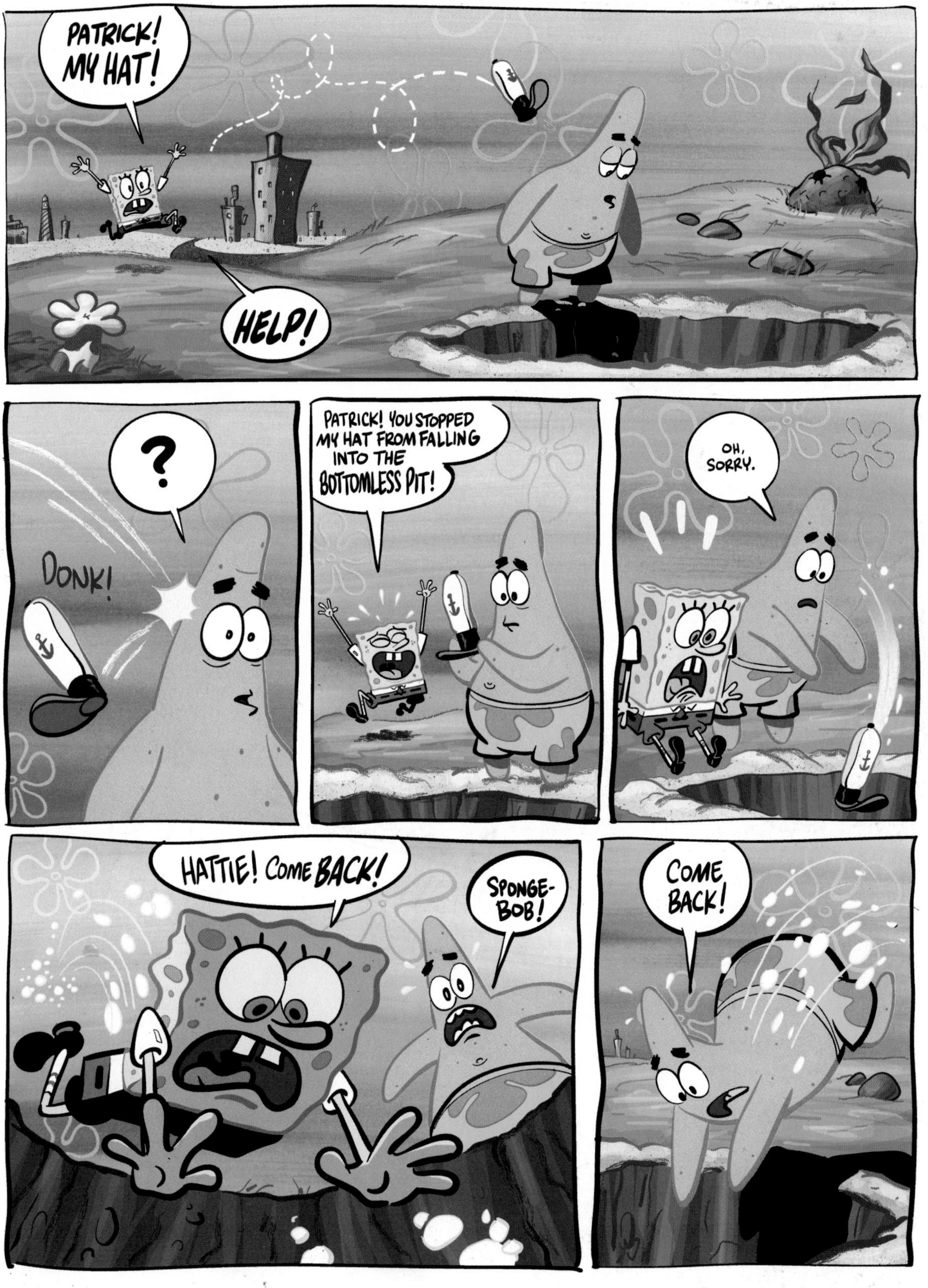
PATRICK! MY HAT!
HELP!
?
DONK!
PATRICK! YOU STOPPED MY HAT FROM FALLING INTO THE BOTTOMLESS PIT!
OH, SORRY.
HATTIE! COME BACK!
SPONGE-BOB!
COME BACK!

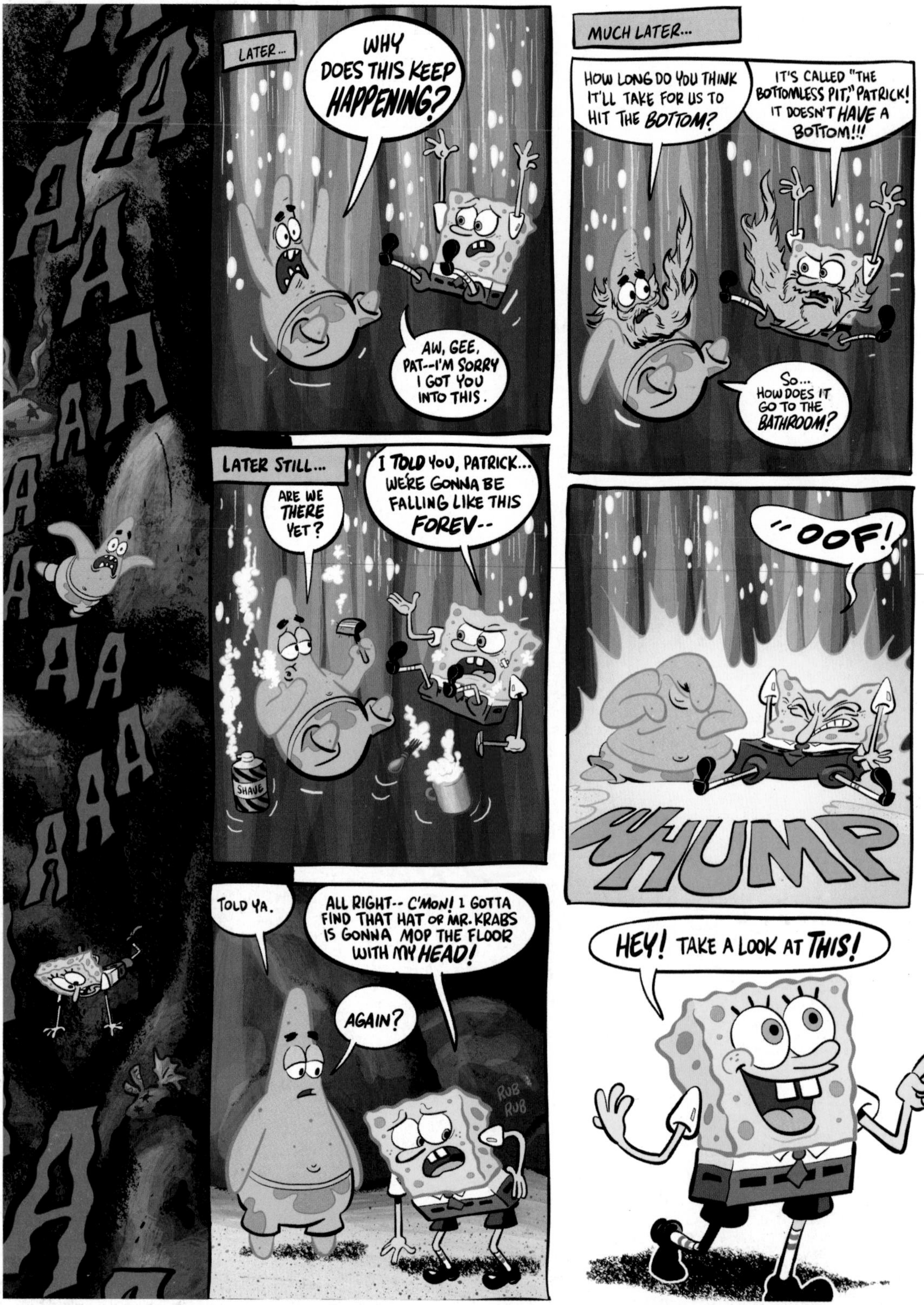

LATER...
WHY DOES THIS KEEP HAPPENING?
AW, GEE, PAT--I'M SORRY I GOT YOU INTO THIS.
MUCH LATER...
HOW LONG DO YOU THINK IT'LL TAKE FOR US TO HIT THE BOTTOM?
IT'S CALLED "THE BOTTOMLESS PIT," PATRICK! IT DOESN'T HAVE A BOTTOM!!!
SO... HOW DOES IT GO TO THE BATHROOM?
LATER STILL...
ARE WE THERE YET?
I TOLD YOU, PATRICK... WE'RE GONNA BE FALLING LIKE THIS FOREV--
SHAVE
--OOF!
WHUMP
TOLD YA.
ALL RIGHT-- C'MON! I GOTTA FIND THAT HAT OR MR. KRABS IS GONNA MOP THE FLOOR WITH MY HEAD!
AGAIN?
RUB RUB
HEY! TAKE A LOOK AT THIS!

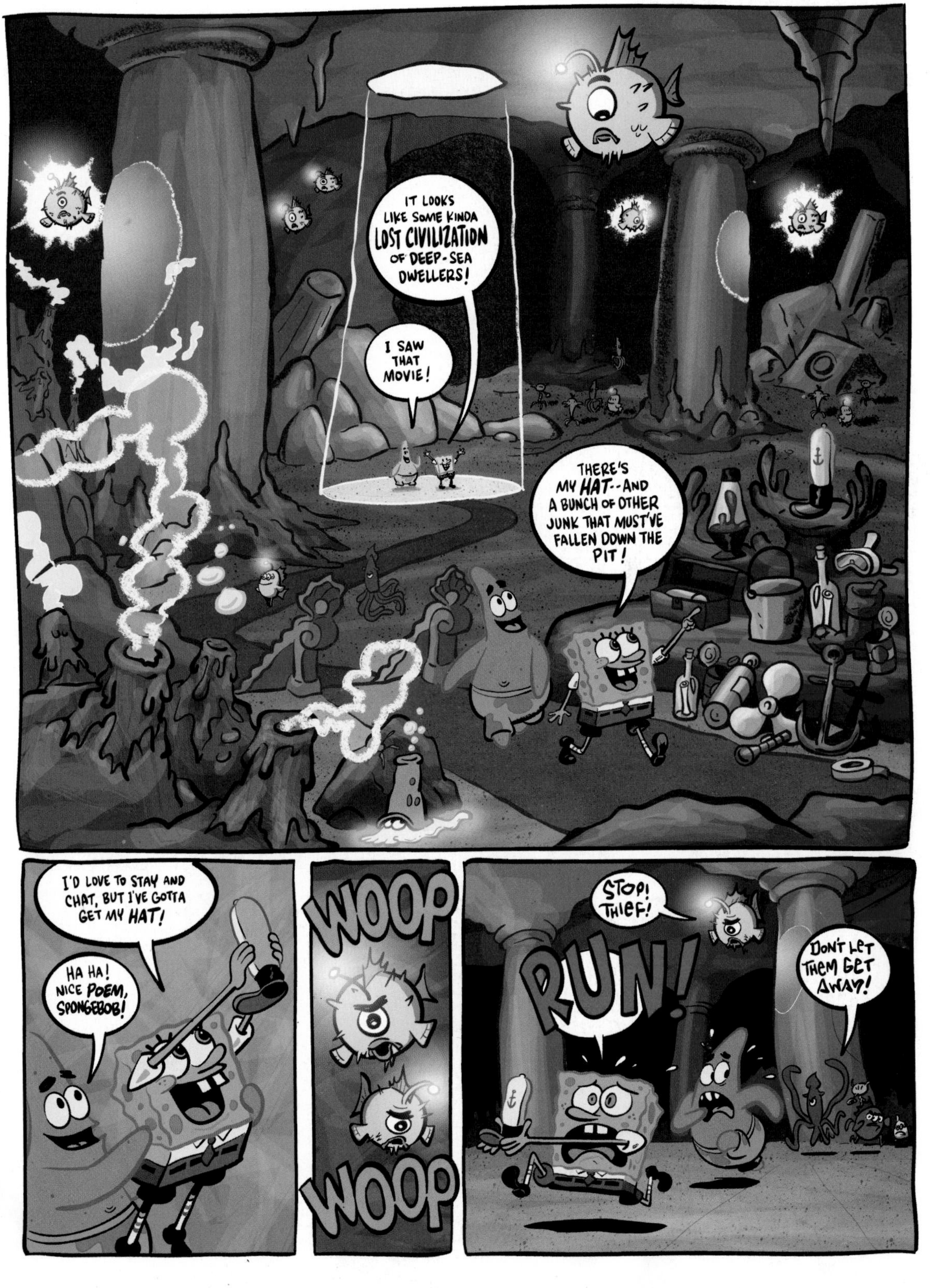
IT LOOKS LIKE SOME KINDA LOST CIVILIZATION OF DEEP-SEA DWELLERS!
I SAW THAT MOVIE!
THERE'S MY HAT--AND A BUNCH OF OTHER JUNK THAT MUST'VE FALLEN DOWN THE PIT!
I'D LOVE TO STAY AND CHAT, BUT I'VE GOTTA GET MY HAT!
HA HA! NICE POEM, SPONGEBOB!
WOOP
WOOP
STOP! THIEF!
RUN!
DON'T LET THEM GET AWAY!

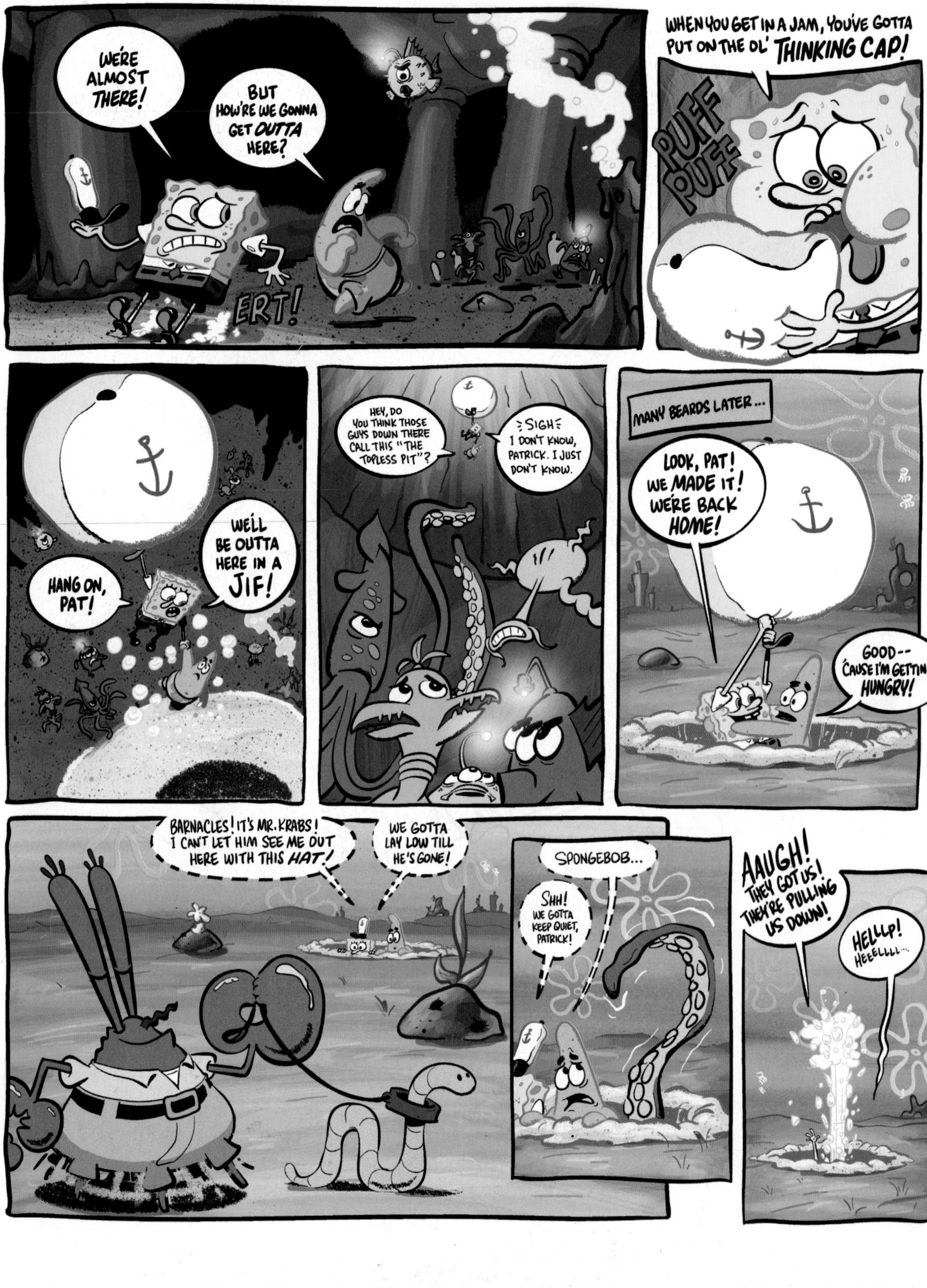
WE'RE ALMOST THERE!
BUT HOW'RE WE GONNA GET OUTTA HERE?
ERT!
WHEN YOU GET IN A JAM, YOU'VE GOTTA PUT ON THE OL' THINKING CAP!
PUFF PUFF
HANG ON, PAT!
WE'LL BE OUTTA HERE IN A JIF!
HEY, DO YOU THINK THOSE GUYS DOWN THERE CALL THIS "THE TOPLESS PIT"?
=SIGH= I DON'T KNOW, PATRICK. I JUST DON'T KNOW.
MANY BEARDS LATER...
LOOK, PAT! WE MADE IT! WE'RE BACK HOME!
GOOD-- 'CAUSE I'M GETTING HUNGRY!
BARNACLES! IT'S MR. KRABS! I CAN'T LET HIM SEE ME OUT HERE WITH THIS HAT!
WE GOTTA LAY LOW TILL HE'S GONE!
SPONGEBOB...
SHH! WE GOTTA KEEP QUIET, PATRICK!
AAUGH! THEY GOT US! THEY'RE PULLING US DOWN!
HELLLP! HEEELLLL...

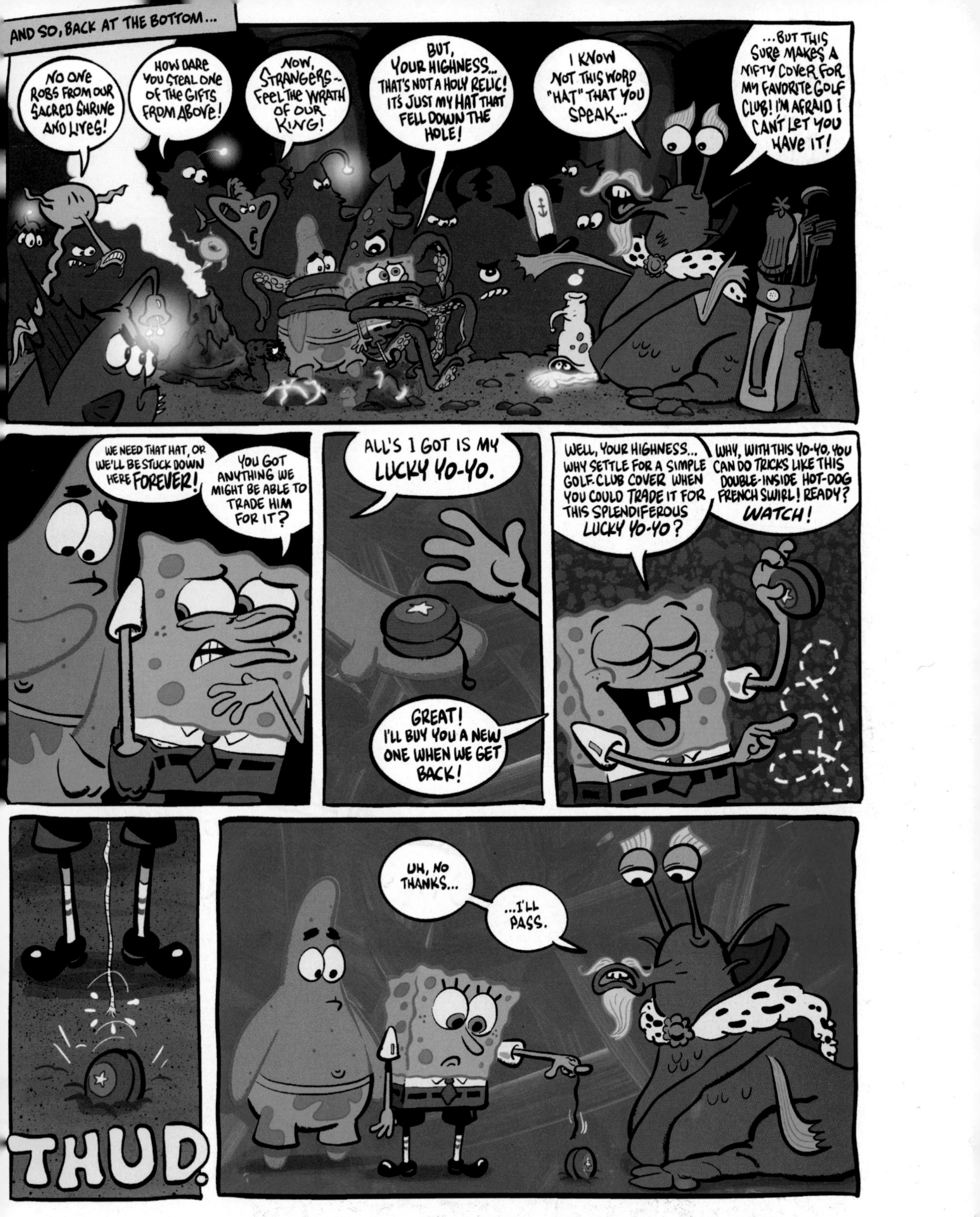
AND SO, BACK AT THE BOTTOM...
NO ONE ROBS FROM OUR SACRED SHRINE AND LIVES!
HOW DARE YOU STEAL ONE OF THE GIFTS FROM ABOVE!
NOW, STRANGERS-- FEEL THE WRATH OF OUR KING!
BUT, YOUR HIGHNESS... THAT'S NOT A HOLY RELIC! IT'S JUST MY HAT THAT FELL DOWN THE HOLE!
I KNOW NOT THIS WORD "HAT" THAT YOU SPEAK...
...BUT THIS SURE MAKES A NIFTY COVER FOR MY FAVORITE GOLF CLUB! I'M AFRAID I CAN'T LET YOU HAVE IT!
WE NEED THAT HAT, OR WE'LL BE STUCK DOWN HERE FOREVER!
YOU GOT ANYTHING WE MIGHT BE ABLE TO TRADE HIM FOR IT?
ALL'S I GOT IS MY LUCKY YO-YO.
GREAT! I'LL BUY YOU A NEW ONE WHEN WE GET BACK!
WELL, YOUR HIGHNESS... WHY SETTLE FOR A SIMPLE GOLF-CLUB COVER WHEN YOU COULD TRADE IT FOR THIS SPLENDIFEROUS LUCKY YO-YO?
WHY, WITH THIS YO-YO, YOU CAN DO TRICKS LIKE THIS DOUBLE-INSIDE HOT-DOG FRENCH SWIRL! READY? WATCH!
THUD.
UH, NO THANKS...
...I'LL PASS.

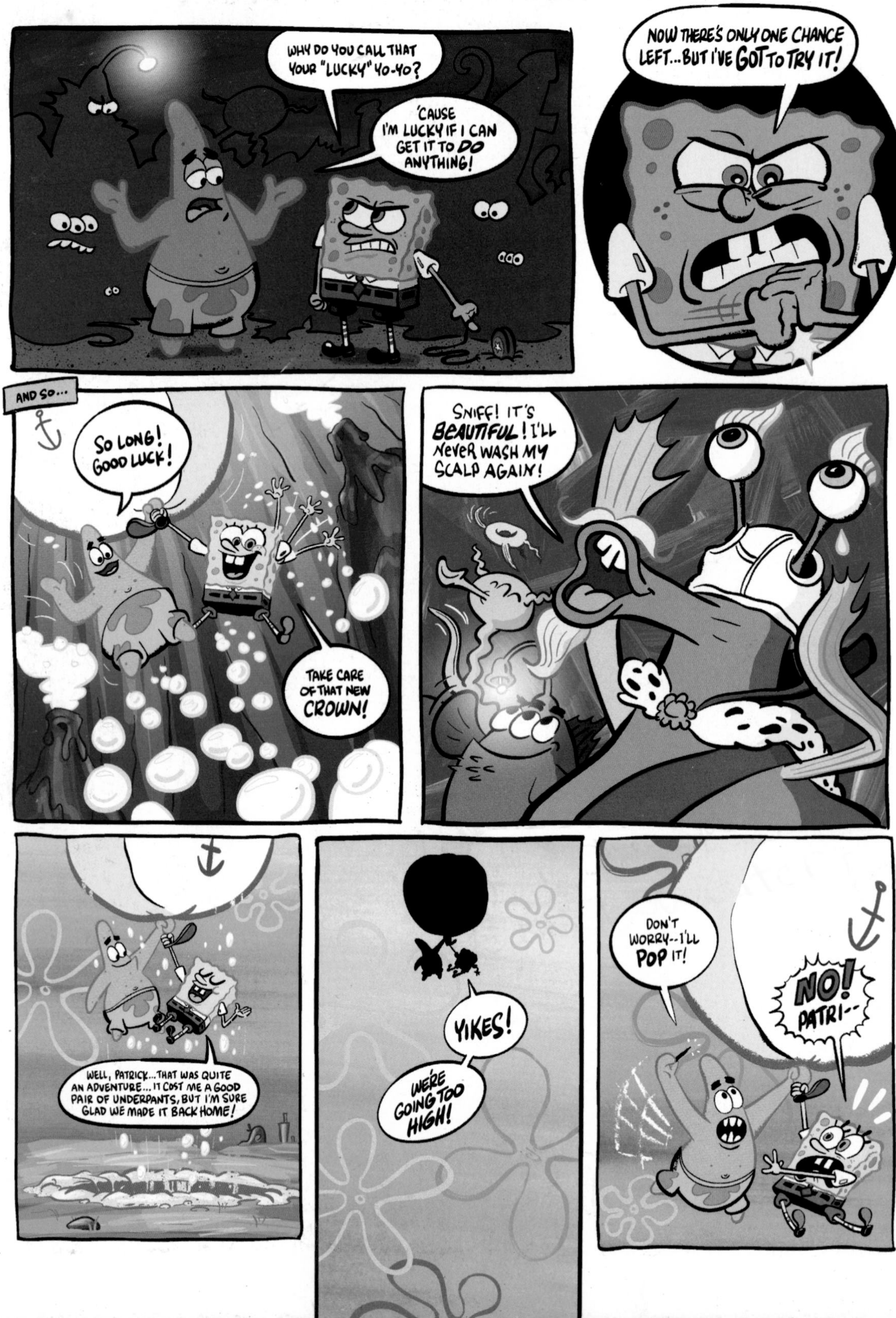

WHY DO YOU CALL THAT YOUR "LUCKY" YO-YO?
'CAUSE I'M LUCKY IF I CAN GET IT TO DO ANYTHING!
NOW THERE'S ONLY ONE CHANCE LEFT... BUT I'VE GOT TO TRY IT!
AND SO...
SO LONG! GOOD LUCK!
TAKE CARE OF THAT NEW CROWN!
SNIFF! IT'S BEAUTIFUL! I'LL NEVER WASH MY SCALP AGAIN!
WELL, PATRICK... THAT WAS QUITE AN ADVENTURE... IT COST ME A GOOD PAIR OF UNDERPANTS, BUT I'M SURE GLAD WE MADE IT BACK HOME!
YIKES!
WE'RE GOING TOO HIGH!
DON'T WORRY--I'LL POP IT!
NO! PATRI--

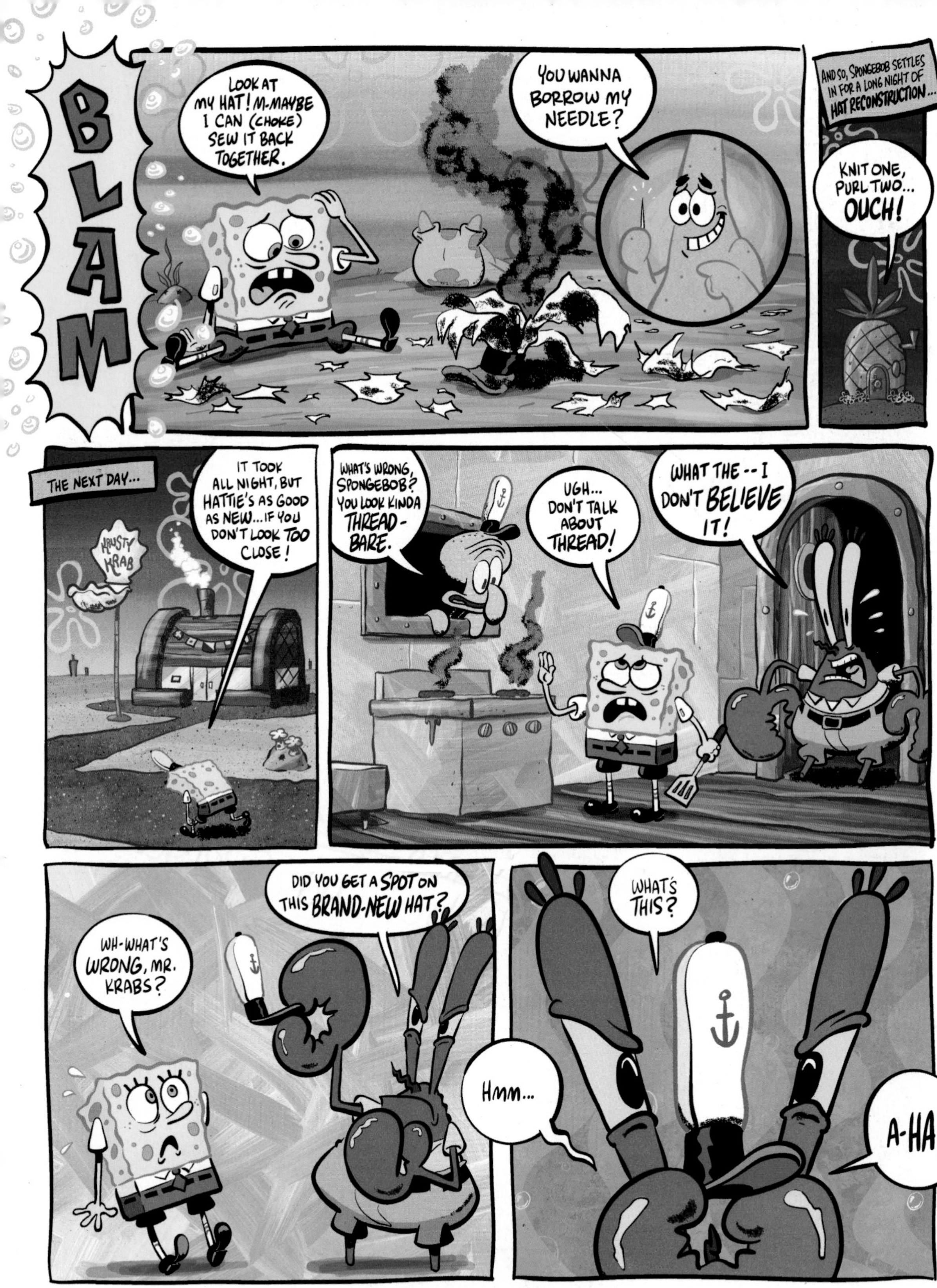
BLAM
LOOK AT MY HAT! M-MAYBE I CAN (CHOKE) SEW IT BACK TOGETHER.
YOU WANNA BORROW MY NEEDLE?
AND SO, SPONGEBOB SETTLES IN FOR A LONG NIGHT OF HAT RECONSTRUCTION...
KNIT ONE, PURL TWO... OUCH!
THE NEXT DAY...
IT TOOK ALL NIGHT, BUT HATTIE'S AS GOOD AS NEW... IF YOU DON'T LOOK TOO CLOSE!
KRUSTY KRAB
WHAT'S WRONG, SPONGEBOB? YOU LOOK KINDA THREAD-BARE.
UGH... DON'T TALK ABOUT THREAD!
WHAT THE -- I DON'T BELIEVE IT!
DID YOU GET A SPOT ON THIS BRAND-NEW HAT?
WH-WHAT'S WRONG, MR. KRABS?
WHAT'S THIS?
HMM...
A-HA!

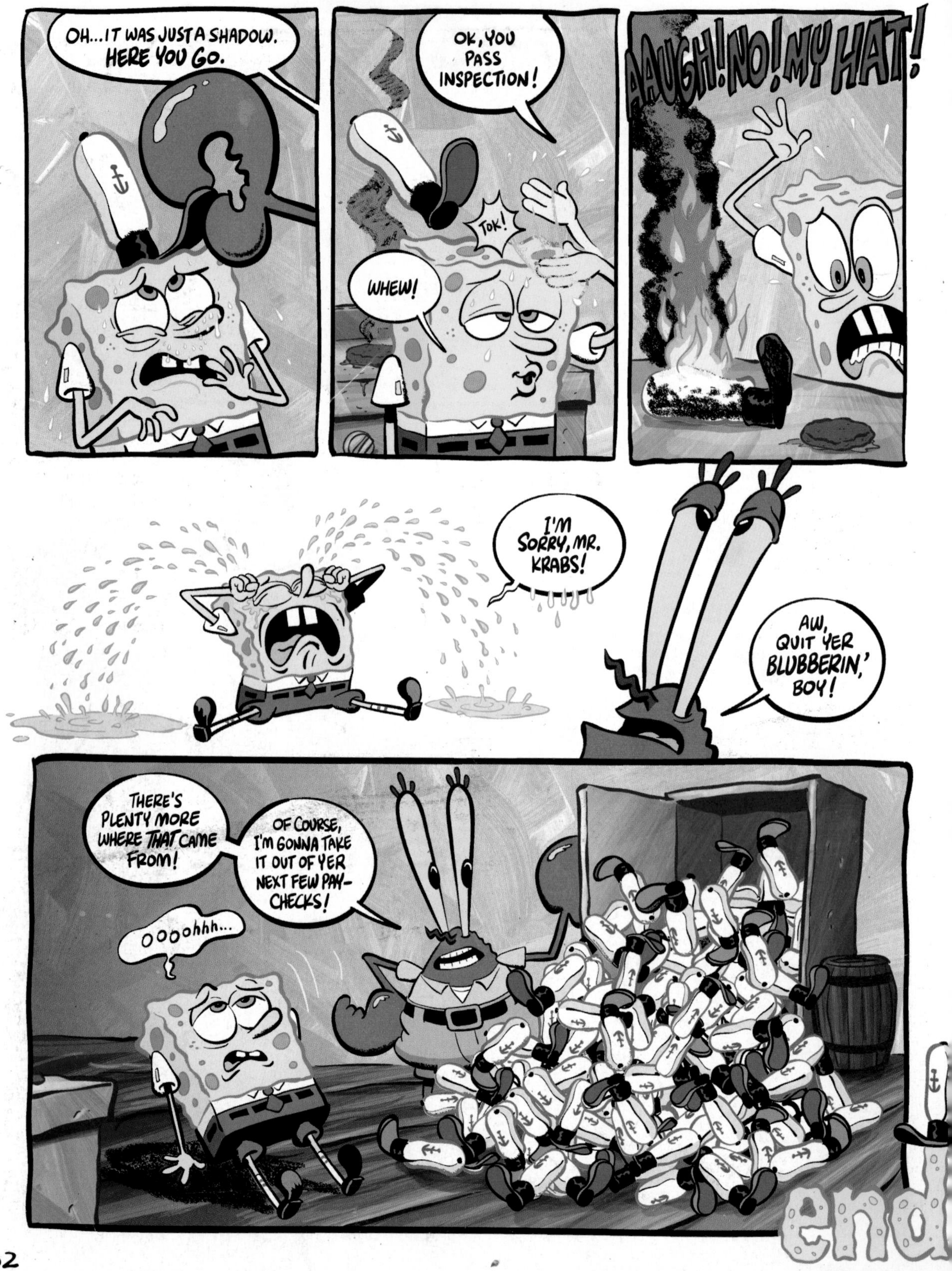
OH...IT WAS JUST A SHADOW. HERE YOU GO.
OK, YOU PASS INSPECTION!
TOK!
WHEW!
AAUGH! NO! MY HAT!
I'M SORRY, MR. KRABS!
AW, QUIT YER BLUBBERIN,' BOY!
THERE'S PLENTY MORE WHERE THAT CAME FROM!
OF COURSE, I'M GONNA TAKE IT OUT OF YER NEXT FEW PAY-CHECKS!
OOOOhhh...
end

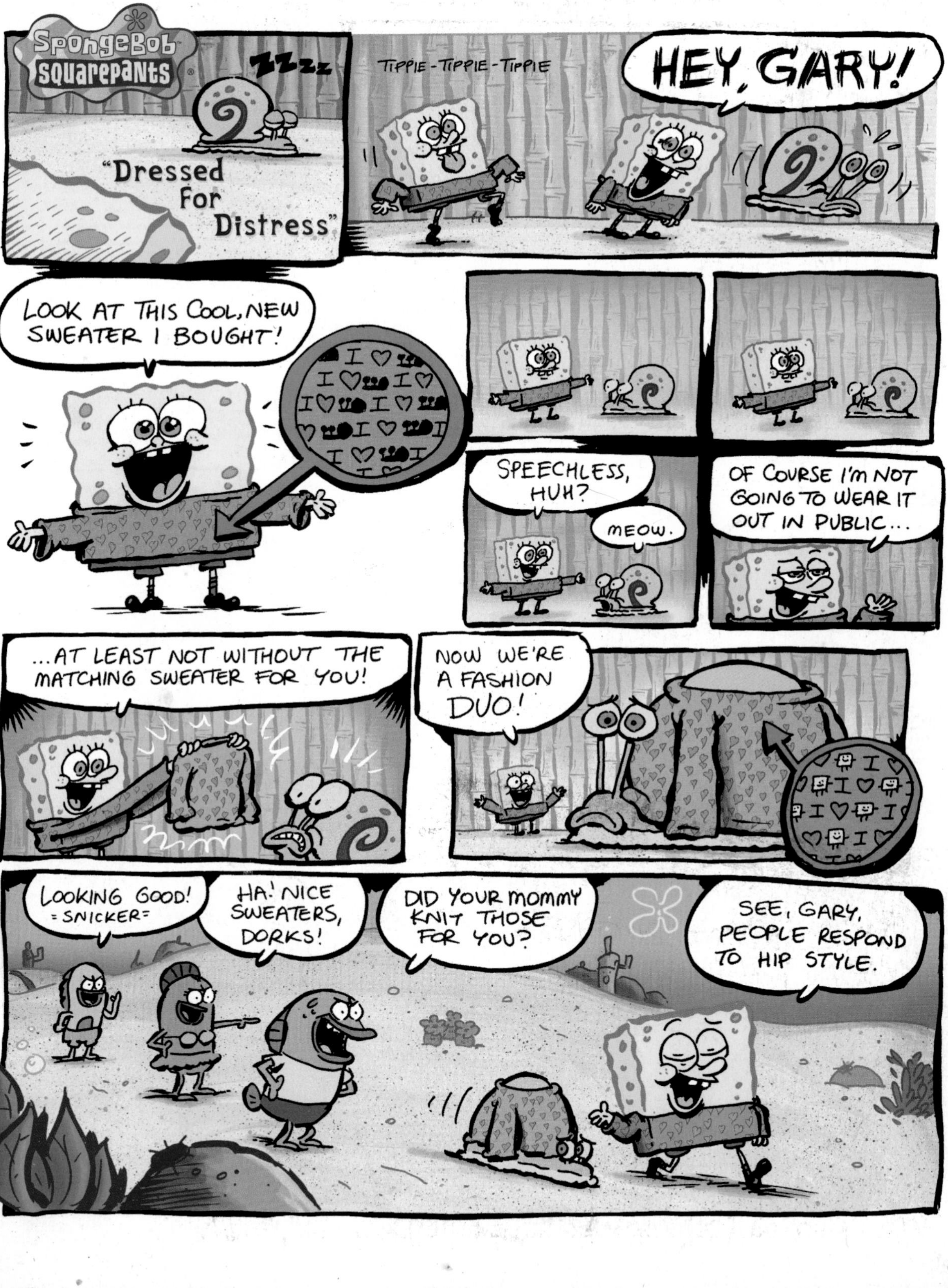
SpongeBob SquarePants
"Dressed For Distress"
ZZZz
TIPPIE - TIPPIE - TIPPIE
HEY, GARY!
LOOK AT THIS COOL, NEW SWEATER I BOUGHT!
SPEECHLESS, HUH?
MEOW.
OF COURSE I'M NOT GOING TO WEAR IT OUT IN PUBLIC...
...AT LEAST NOT WITHOUT THE MATCHING SWEATER FOR YOU!
NOW WE'RE A FASHION DUO!
LOOKING GOOD! =SNICKER=
HA! NICE SWEATERS, DORKS!
DID YOUR MOMMY KNIT THOSE FOR YOU?
SEE, GARY, PEOPLE RESPOND TO HIP STYLE.

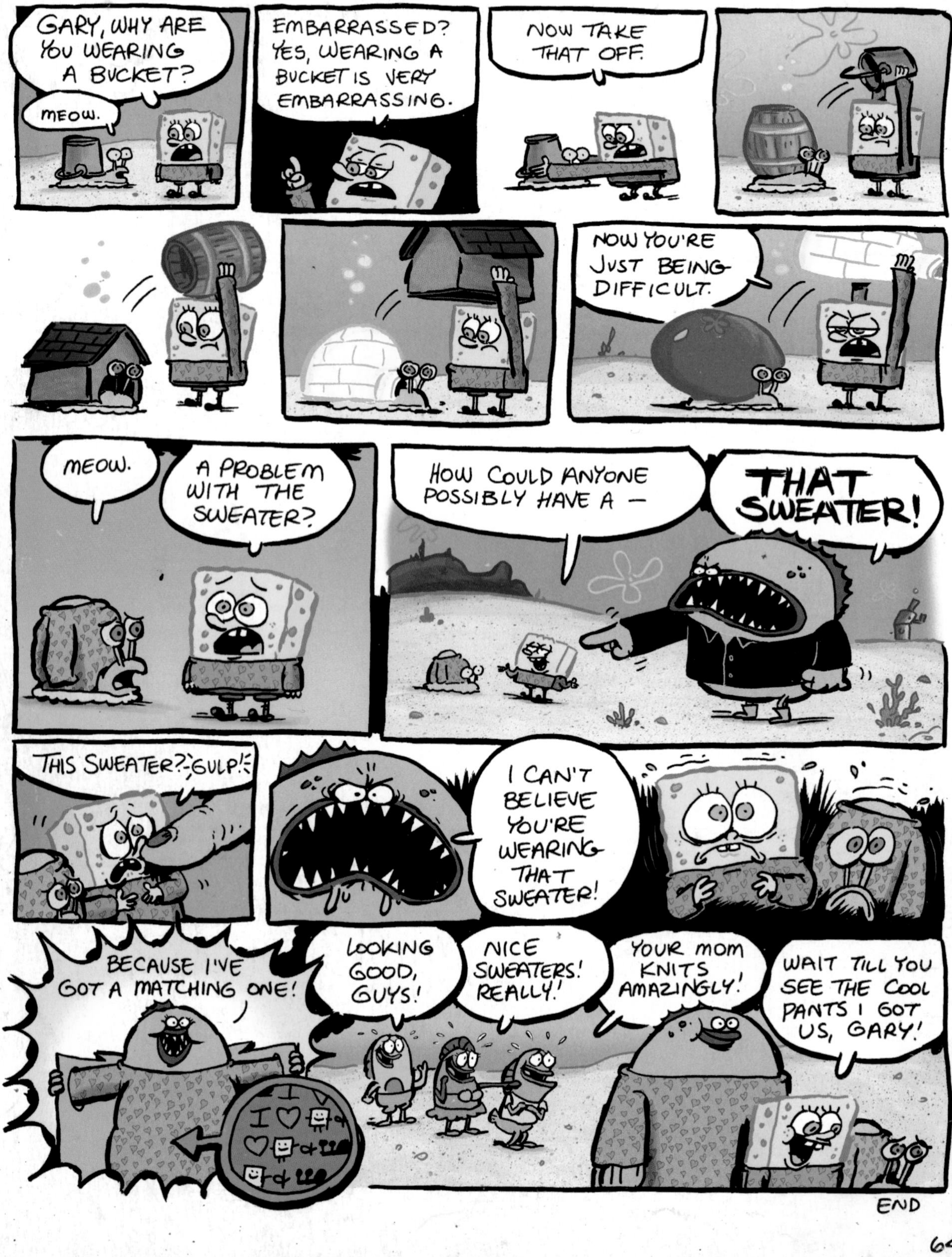
GARY, WHY ARE YOU WEARING A BUCKET?
MEOW.
EMBARRASSED? YES, WEARING A BUCKET IS VERY EMBARRASSING.
NOW TAKE THAT OFF.
NOW YOU'RE JUST BEING DIFFICULT.
MEOW.
A PROBLEM WITH THE SWEATER?
HOW COULD ANYONE POSSIBLY HAVE A —
THAT SWEATER!
THIS SWEATER? GULP!
I CAN'T BELIEVE YOU'RE WEARING THAT SWEATER!
BECAUSE I'VE GOT A MATCHING ONE!
LOOKING GOOD, GUYS!
NICE SWEATERS! REALLY!
YOUR MOM KNITS AMAZINGLY!
WAIT TILL YOU SEE THE COOL PANTS I GOT US, GARY!
END